The Masters Review

ten stories

Best Emerging Writers 2025

To receive new fiction, contest deadlines,
and other curated content right to your inbox,
send an email to newsletter@mastersreview.com

The Masters Review

ten stories

Best Emerging Writers 2025

Danielle Sherman • Sena Moon

Amy Wilde • Katie Henken Robinson

Stephenjohn Holgate • Amelia Christmas Gramling

Cristina Chira • Liz Rose Shulman

Katerina Ivanov Prado • J. Stillwell Powers

Stories Selected by
Andrew Porter

RED MARE
PRESS

Contents

When I was in graduate school, I remember one of my professors, Frank Conroy, saying to a classroom of students that he could tell a piece of fiction was good when he could sense a soul on the other side of the words. Frank dispensed little pieces of writerly wisdom often, but this statement had a profound impact on me at the time, in part because it explained to me in a very simple but clear way why it was I loved certain short stories and certain short story writers. It wasn't about style or subject matter or even plot. It was about a very intimate connection that I was having with the characters on the other side of the story's words. It was that simple. It was about connecting with another soul. When I didn't feel that connection—perhaps the story was more interested in being stylistically slick or clever—I'd find myself putting the story down and moving on to something else. But when I did feel it, that story would become like a house that I wanted to live inside, that I wanted to read over and over again in hopes of rediscovering the feeling it gave me the first time I read it.

Choosing the pieces from this exceptional shortlist has proved to be so much more difficult than I'd imagined, in part because all thirty of the stories and essays on the shortlist fit Frank's criteria for a good piece of writing in one way or another, and with each one of them I could see a strong case being made for that story or essay's inclusion. In the end, though, the pieces that I ended up choosing were the pieces that grabbed ahold of me from the first sentence and didn't let go, that continued to linger in my mind days and weeks later, that continued to haunt me.

Among this eclectic group of stories and essays I can now see certain recurring themes: romantic and familial relationships, issues of identity, the navigation of complex power dynamics, coping with physical illness and the ways our bodies fail us, trauma in its many forms, physical and metaphorical displacement, and so on. These stories are also bonded by the clarity and elegance of these writers' sentences, by their vivid and immersive descriptions of place, by their psychological and emotional depth, and, of course, in many cases, by their humor and wit. As challenging as some of the subject matter in these pieces is, these stories and essays are also filled with light: with humor and hope, with kindness and forgiveness.

Interestingly, one of the most prominent themes I noticed among these pieces was a focus on the uncertainty of the future, something that struck me as intriguing given the uncertainty that so many people in our country are feeling right now about our own collective future. Of course, maybe that feeling of uncertainty is something that's simply baked into the DNA of the short story and personal essay forms. Or perhaps uncertainty is something I'm simply drawn to myself as a reader. Maybe the prominence of uncertainty in these pieces says more about me than it does about the pieces I chose or the writers who submitted them.

I'm not sure that I have the answer to these questions, but what I do know for certain is that after reading the thirty short stories and essays on the contest's shortlist I can tell that the futures of the American short story and essay are very bright. And in the face of whatever uncertainty people might be feeling in their lives right now, the art being made during this time is very affirming, affirming if for no other reason than the fact that it is so very good. And the stories and essays in these pages are all incredibly good. Every one of them will delight you, surprise you, and will remind you, most of all, of what all good literature does: that there are other souls out there in the world just like you, struggling with adversities and doing their best, that none of us here is truly alone.

—Andrew Porter
Guest Judge

Reach Out

Danielle Sherman

Minori's extraction is tomorrow, and so Sarah has listened to records all day. Even as Sarah moves about the apartment kitchen, leaning so close over the oven its heat should sting her face, the music still reaches her through the walls of the other room. She only steps back into the living room to turn off the sound when she sees the school bus out the window.

Through the glass, she watches Minori hop off the bus, wave to the driver with a small, gloved hand. Minori is barely fourteen, and looks twelve. The sight of her reminds Sarah of how early providers schedule extractions these days; students didn't undergo extractions until their late teens back in her school years, though that was nearly a decade ago. Minori's bright, open face looks younger than ever as she taps three polite knocks on Sarah's door.

Sarah opens it; for a few moments, she and Minori look at each other. Minori wears her earnestness like a second coat. Sarah does too. They each know that the other is trying to seem brave.

The school bus slowly pulls away to resume its route, bearing the words "Rock Creek Preparatory Academy" in formal blue font on its side. Minori has now ridden it for the last time. After her extraction, she will not return to school, nor Sarah's apartment.

She will spend the whole of each day in her group home, learning to adjust, and when she turns eighteen she will live on her own. That means four years of waiting, four years of helping the home supervisor attend to the rest of the children.

Sarah wonders if today Minori said goodbye to her friends who live in other group homes, the friends she will no longer see now that she has left school for good. She wonders if Minori has any friends to say goodbye to at all. Sarah had none, on her last day. Her classmates who knew of her imminent extraction only avoided eye contact, half-disdainful and half-pitying, but then again they had always done that.

Sarah shuts the door, taking care to watch her hand grasp the knob so that she knows she has actually closed it, and asks Minori how her day was.

"Good," is all Minori says as she places her backpack by the door. It likely carries toiletries, a change of clothes; Minori's supervisor allowed her to stay overnight, just this once, per the girl's request. "Thank you for having me, Miss June."

"Sarah," she corrects, as she always does. Minori stands blinking and unsure, as if waiting for instructions. Sarah gestures toward the dining table. "Are you ready?"

Closed-mouth, weight on her heels, Minori shakes her head.

Something wrenches within Sarah: deep, the only place she can sense the feeling. "For dinner, I mean. I made you your favorite."

"Oh." Minori stands a little straighter. It is too late: Sarah cannot unsee the way she darkened at the question, seemed to fold herself into a smaller shape. It will be a long night.

*   *   *

No one made Sarah's favorite meal the night before she lost her sense of touch. No one else had undergone that particular extraction, at least no one affiliated with her preparatory school. She had been the first and only of Rock Creek's students in that regard. Until Minori. Like Minori, Sarah lived in a group home with students awaiting taste-smell extraction. Unlike Minori, Sarah had no predecessor to advise her.

She remembers when the Rock Creek recruiter had sat at this very dining table and told her about Minori. She remembers what she had made, too: steamed mushrooms and asparagus over a bed of jasmine rice, laden with garlic and butter. The recruiter finished her plate by the time Sarah swallowed five bites. Sarah always takes a long time to chew; her teeth cannot detect if they have ground the food enough.

The recruiter wiped her mouth delicately, deftly, with a clean white napkin. "We have another student in our program who will contribute toward a touch restoration," she explained. That was how Rock Creek staff phrased such things. "Her extraction date has just been scheduled three months from now."

First the recruiter asked Sarah to teach a class at Rock Creek, and she said no. Then the recruiter asked her to be a supervisor, and she said no to that too.

"I don't want to manage a group home," Sarah told her. "I don't want to step foot in that school again."

"Research has shown that students feel better adjusted post-extraction when they take preparatory classes beforehand," the recruiter pressed. "That is the point of Rock Creek, after all."

Sarah studied the woman's suit of navy blue: the same color as the students' uniforms. She had heard that selling point countless times before, from teachers and supervisors and older students. She was tired of hearing it. Where was Sarah's preparation, then? Other students learned sign language, braille, walked the halls with silencing headphones or practiced with white canes—and she had sat in the library with no specialized lessons to attend. Other students shared bedrooms in their group homes, spent evenings playing card games—and Sarah lay alone in her designated corner of the house, listening to the sounds of the taste-smell kids whispering in the other rooms and the branch of a honey locust tree knocking against her window.

"Think of how much someone like that would've helped you then," the recruiter said, as if reading her thoughts. "You could be the mentor you wish you had."

"I want nothing to do with the program. I've had my extraction. I'm done."

"You'd be compensated."

"I don't want your money."

Which wasn't quite true, because Sarah still collects checks every month: her "pension," Rock Creek calls it, her due for the product she had sold. Hearing and sight extraction pensions last for about seven years, taste-smell pensions for four. Touch extraction pays for twelve. Sarah didn't need a salary, not then.

But she knew, and the recruiter knew, that the pension would run out one day. Sarah had begun to pick up occasional sign language interpreter jobs to prepare for that eventuality, but the money she earned from them would not be enough on its own. All her teachers and supervisors had once been students who, unprepared for any other kind of employment, returned to Rock Creek when the well ran dry. The system is sheltered, seamless, a snake eating its own tail.

But Sarah did not acknowledge this, and the recruiter did not point it out—only smiled, calmly, as if to say that she could be patient, that she could wait, that she would be back when circumstances inevitably changed.

Sarah stood up to take her plate.

*   *   *

Tonight Sarah has made yams with marshmallows. Minori likes sweet things. But she eats even slower than Sarah as they sit silently at the dining table. Sarah chews—methodically, carefully, mindful not to bite her tongue—while Minori pushes at her food with a fork.

Usually Minori devours these dinners, despite Sarah's urging to practice taking small, hesitant bites. Those previous nights, as Minori hunched over the plate, teeth flashing, Sarah would think of Miriam's same unrepentant eagerness, same hunger. Then she'd forget to tell Minori to slow down.

Minori normally loves Sarah's cooking for the same reason Sarah loves to make it: in the group home, the taste-smell kids only ate bland, beige oatmeal and hard bread and watery smoothies.

Nothing that would give them a flavor or aroma to miss. That was the cornerstone of Rock Creek's philosophy: the less children used the sense they would someday live without, the easier the transition would be. The practice followed the children home from school, where the supervisors enforced it just as emphatically as their teachers.

The supervisor at Sarah's home didn't make separate meals for her, so she had spent eighteen years eating tofu and burning scentless candles. Minori had described something similar.

"I'm done," Minori says softly, setting down her fork. It clinks against her plate; Sarah sees the gloved hand trembling. She takes Minori's dishes to the kitchen without scolding her for not eating more.

She returns to the dining room to find Minori holding her head higher, hands squeezing each other in her lap, like she's steeled herself for something. "I want to know what will happen tomorrow," Minori says.

Sarah takes her time sitting down. Then: "A school van will be here to pick us up at nine. It'll drive us to the extraction clinic, and afterward it'll drop you off at the group home."

"No," says Minori, her voice the smallest thing about her now. "I want to know what will happen."

"I'll be there when you wake up," Sarah says. It is the one thing she can promise.

"They'll put me to sleep?"

"Yes, they'll put you to sleep."

They've been over this several times in the past few months, but Minori always asks the same questions. "And when I wake up, I won't feel anything?"

"That's right."

"And I won't feel anything ever again?"

The cold clinic room. The rough texture of the hospital bed linens. The lack of the rough texture of the hospital bed linens. Sarah closes her eyes before the memory slips under her skin and crawls deep, before she is back there again. "That's right."

"Okay." Minori walks two purple-clad fingers through the air, hovering them just above the tablecloth. "Is there a chance I could die?"

"No." Sarah has heard stories of extractions gone wrong: an error in the procedure rendering the sense too damaged to successfully reimplant in the restoration patient who paid to receive it. Then the student loses part of themselves for no reason, and is not entitled to compensation. But she does not tell this to Minori.

Minori's fingers pause, and she lifts her wide, dark eyes toward Sarah. "Why can't I go home with you?" she asks. "Why do I have to go back to the group home? I could stay here."

Sarah folds her own gloved hands around each other, a habit she unconsciously developed back at school and sometimes still enacts despite the lack of comfort, one that Minori has picked up from her. "I'm not a supervisor," she says gently, firmly. "I can't care for you."

"But you teach me anyway," says Minori.

"We have weekly lessons. That's different."

Minori does not reply. This is how the conversation always ends. But this time, as Sarah stands to clear her own plate from the table, Minori asks, "Do they make you live alone?"

A plate tips in Sarah's arms. She clutches it tighter, too tight, and a tiny fissure blooms at its porcelain edge. She cannot decide whether the question is genuine or Minori just wants to lash out; she tastes the bitter undertones of the girl's words, a hint of cruelty that makes her think of Miriam again. It is not just the names that run together—it is Miriam's latent edge, Miriam's self-defensive bite that Sarah senses within Minori.

"There aren't any rules about that," Sarah says. "This is just how I've chosen to live." She carries the plate into the kitchen.

"I'm going to live with my sister," Minori says from behind her. "My older sister. I know I have one because I've dreamed of her. I'll find her someday, and we'll live together."

Minori has never told Sarah of a sister or of her dreams. "Come help me dry the dishes," Sarah tells her.

So Minori falls silent again, dutifully drying plates and pots with her still-shaking hands. Sarah removes her own gloves to do the washing. She does not allow Minori to use hot water here—even when the girl showers, it must be cold. Soon enough Minori will never be able to feel warmth like that again. It is better if she never feels it in the first place.

*   *   *

Miriam told Sarah about the rumors of extractions gone awry. She had found Sarah in the library while skipping lip reading lessons; she liked to ask her teachers to use the bathroom and then wander around the halls.

She said hello to Sarah, who shushed her. Miriam was not supposed to speak unless she absolutely had to, and she was not allowed to take off her silencing headphones outside of class.

Sarah tried pointing at the noise-cancellers hanging around her neck, but Miriam moved as if to bat away her hands, so she withdrew. "Cut that out," Miriam said, laughing, and her voice was dark and gravelly from lack of use. Sarah always liked hearing Miriam's voice, even though it meant she was breaking the rules.

After Miriam finished telling her all the extraction horror stories she knew, she paused and aimed a kick at the legs of Sarah's chair. "Where do they tell you your sense of touch will end up?"

"A war veteran. Someone wounded in combat who got nerve damage somewhere." Her supervisor had told her that, and she'd felt proud; that assurance, the knowledge of her usefulness, was a warm thing she kept in her uniform pocket, something to take out and hold whenever she lay sleepless with fear in her solitary bedroom.

But Miriam only threw her head back and laughed, harder this time. "That's bullshit, Sarah. You know that's not where it's going."

She felt her face flush—she could feel such things back then, at sixteen. "Where, then?"

"To some lady whose Botox got botched. Speaking of messed up procedures. That's the only kind of person who can afford something like feeling restoration."

"Really?"

Miriam nodded, her mouth twisted into a closed smile. The smile bore no cruelty, just mirth; Sarah believed her. She had met Miriam December in sign language class, which she had asked to take just to fill her schedule given that she had no other required courses beyond basic writing and math. Her seat was next to Miriam's—Miriam with her short black curls, her wire frame glasses. Her chapped lips that made Sarah's own mouth prickle. At first glance she struck Sarah as a girl who knew things, a girl whose supervisor often snapped at her for breaking objects just to hear what sound they'd make. The other students in their class—especially the ones from her group home—avoided Miriam for such reasons, just as they avoided Sarah for others.

You don't know that for sure, Sarah signed, even though she knew Miriam was right. She signed so that Miriam would stop talking.

But Miriam answered aloud, "Don't kid yourself. That's how it works. It's why our parents or mothers or whoever sent us here. That's the deal."

Sarah pretended to return to her math homework, the once-warm thing crumbling into cinders in her pocket. She had never liked the word "parents." She had always thought of them as vague, faceless figures that had signed her away at the city hospital where she'd been born. The ones that did not want her. The ones that, presented with four different extraction options, had chosen the most extreme, the most rare.

Her supervisor had told her that parents did this with good intentions, that they chose to secure housing and education and income for a child they could not care for. But, Sarah knew, supervisors often lied.

Miriam stood watching Sarah ignore her until the librarian stalked over to tell her to get back to class. She slipped away, turning once to shoot a grin over her shoulder. Miriam's right hand flicked two fingers outward from her eyes, pointed, and then extended the same two fingers with the thumb curving up: *See you later.*

*   *   *

Minori breaks her silence to tell Sarah her record is still spinning. She must have muted the volume but forgotten to stop the machine. Sarah cautiously lifts the needle and guides the LP back into its sleeve. Shelves of them line her living room, carefully arranged and free of dust.

Minori's eyes rove across the titles as she stands among the couch and chairs. Her arms hang limply; her gaze is vague and far away, music from another room.

"Do you want to listen to some?" Sarah offers.

Minori stretches a hand toward one shelf, and then tucks it back in her pocket. "Can we watch a movie?"

"Of course we can." Whatever she wants. Sarah sits in the armchair nearest the sofa while Minori points the remote at the television screen and clicks through channels. Huddled on the cushions with the bright folds of her coat unfurling around her, the girl resembles a flower mid-bloom.

The coat and the gloves were Minori's first lesson. As soon as the Rock Creek recruiter introduced them and then left, Sarah took Minori to the city. She rarely ever visited, usually avoided the crowds of people and crush of buildings, but she led Minori straight out of the subway and into a clothing store.

"I'm going to get you a big coat, and a pair of nice gloves," Sarah told her. "Don't lose them, and don't take them off. Not even to eat, or when it's hot—only when you have to. Understand?"

Minori nodded.

"What's your favorite color?"

Minori wanted purple. She told Sarah how that morning, on the ride from the group home to Sarah's apartment, she'd seen a beautiful little house with a plum-painted door. She said she liked that the door was allowed to look so much brighter than the doors of all the other houses around it. "Once I leave my group home," Minori said, "that's the house I want to live in."

So Sarah searched the store for purple, skirting wide arcs around other shoppers, with Minori drifting at her heels. Sometimes the girl would try to sidle up beside her, pressing close, and always Sarah took one quick step aside.

Once she found some items, she had Minori try them on alone in the changing room. Sarah waited outside, eyeing her reflection in the floor-length mirror. The woman she saw was pale and stiff-shouldered and not nearly up to the task of preparing this child for what lay ahead. She sat in the chair too gingerly, as if unsure it would hold her weight. Her gloves were maroon.

The clothes were a trick she had thought of after her own extraction. The idea was to layer and layer and layer, to put as many barriers as possible between her skin and whatever might come into contact with it. That way, when she touched something and didn't feel it, her mind could attribute it to the intervening fabrics. They worked as a kind of excuse.

She had gotten the idea from the stories Miriam had told her of certain students recovering from sight extraction who continued to keep the surgical bandages over their eyes for months after the operation. "If they never remove the bandages," Miriam explained, "they can blame the darkness on the blindfold, instead of the other thing."

Minori emerged from the dressing room back in her blue uniform, the purple fabrics gathered in her arms. She said she was satisfied with her selections. "But the coat is a little itchy," she added. Sarah did not point out that soon enough it would cease to be a problem.

"I'm glad you like them," Sarah said. "These are my gifts to you. They'll help get you ready, and they'll help you adjust afterwards. I'll explain it on the way back."

Minori nodded slowly. She slipped her hands into her gloves—deep, royal purple, the color of the bruises that surfaced on Sarah's skin in the months after her extraction, when she frequently knocked into things without noticing. "Thank you, Miss June," she whispered solemnly.

Sarah flinched. She hated that surname, hated the lazy way Rock Creek designated each student by the month they had been born and then surrendered to the school. "Please call me Sarah," she said.

Now Sarah watches Minori lower the remote, fixate on the film flickering across the screen, and tug at the coat sleeve that slipped over her hand. Someday she will grow into it. For now it seems to swallow her whole.

*   *   *

Once, while looking out the bus window, Miriam asked Sarah if she would still feel pain after her extraction.

Sarah had just boarded. The Rock Creek bus had picked up her and the taste-smell kids on its route to the school campus. It lingered outside her group home as the students found their seats. Sarah followed Miriam's gaze toward the two-story house hunkered in the shade of the surrounding trees. One of them, the honey locust, thrust its branches against the window of her upstairs bedroom. Miriam was staring at its long, wicked spines.

"I don't know," Sarah answered honestly.

"Your supervisor never told you?"

"My supervisor doesn't know either. There's no one here that knows what it's like." Later Sarah will learn that the answer is yes—but like any other sensation, she will experience it only in a vague sense. It will seem hidden and abstract, never on the surface of her skin; she will dimly register the thing somewhere in her brain more than she will truly feel it. As if her body is a cave and the feeling exists somewhere deep, deep inside.

"No one that will tell you, you mean," said Miriam.

"It's not like that," Sarah said, a little more forcefully than she meant to. "Not everything is some grand conspiracy, Miriam."

The bus pulled away and her group home slid out of sight.

"But think about it. Even if you're the first from Rock Creek… I mean, there's other schools. And the city's so big. Why isn't anyone like you at least teaching here? Why won't any of them be your super—"

"Because they don't have to be," Sarah snapped. "They can work. They find jobs."

Miriam went quiet. She began to slide her thumb back and forth across the tender skin of her own wrist with such gentleness that, watching her, Sarah immediately regretted what she had said.

But what she had said was true. Sarah's own supervisor had explained it to her and all the taste-smell kids in the group home: They could go out into the world, after everything was over—those were the words the supervisor used—and they stood a chance of getting hired. The sight kids and the hearing kids did not. Their loss was too debilitating, despite all of Rock Creek's preparation. And it was too visible. At best they could become teachers or supervisors, but they would not escape the school. Sarah could—at least they assumed she could. When Sarah had first joined her sign language class, the hearing students' resentful stares grated against her skin. They did not make room for her at their tables, did not move their backpacks from unoccupied chairs. Sarah found the sole empty seat beside the only other girl no one turned toward to practice their conversational signing. And Sarah found that girl to be the only person who did not look at her with envy and revulsion.

But now the girl did.

"I don't like talking about it," Sarah said quietly. "But you asked." Her hands clung together in her lap. Preparatory academies produced so many taste-smell suppliers that at least a handful of such students returned to work for those same schools. But touch restoration was nearly unheard of then, and so Sarah was alone.

She risked a glance toward Miriam. Her glasses looked dirty. Sarah wanted to clean them. She brushed her fingertips along the lenses—not Miriam's face, but the windows to her face. Miriam's eyes shifted toward her and Sarah, remembering herself, drew her hand back into her lap.

Miriam adjusted her glasses. "If I were you," she said, "I'd touch everything I could before my extraction. Just to know what every texture feels like before it's too late. Satin and chalkboards and grass—even that thorny tree."

A laugh—part relief and part derision—ripped from Sarah's mouth. "I hope you're joking." Sarah avoided busy hallways out of fear of bumping into some other student, fitted her bed with the most threadbare sheets in the group home, had already begun to shower with cold water. No one had told her to do these things, and it didn't stop the other kids in her group home from pinching her under tables or sliding their fingers against the back of her neck for the pleasure of watching her writhe away. But she couldn't think of any other ways to prepare.

"I'm not," Miriam said. A girl in the seat behind them leaned over, held a finger to her lips, then jabbed it toward Miriam's headphones. But Miriam ignored her, steadily holding Sarah's gaze through the smudged lens of her glasses. "I'm not."

*   *   *

Not long after that conversation on the bus, Miriam found Sarah in the library again. *Come with me*, she signed. *I want to show you something.*

Sarah glanced around for the librarian: Miriam was being discreet, which worried her. Miriam waved a hand in front of her eyes to catch her attention, and then added, *Not much time. Supposed to be in the bathroom.*

She led Sarah through unfamiliar halls and down staff-only stairs; they stopped before an unlabeled door positioned between rooms usually reserved for teacher meetings. Miriam opened it and ushered her inside.

The lights barely worked; their dimness cast the room in an eerie, twilight glow when Miriam shut the door to the hallway. Still Sarah could discern the array of objects strewn across the desks: water-damaged textbooks, glasses with cracked tinted lenses, the pieces of a deconstructed camera.

Miriam hunched over a cardboard box in the corner. "This stays between us, okay?" She stood, unsheathing a black disk out of some kind of folder, and picked her way across the room until she reached a device Sarah vaguely recognized.

"What is that?"

"Watch." Miriam placed the disk on the machine and touched a metal arm to its surface. She pressed a button, and the disk began to spin.

Then Sarah realized what the device was, although no sound came out of it yet. Her nerves crackled with alarm. "Miriam. No."

"It's being difficult. Hold on." Miriam leaned over the record player. Her eyelashes swept against the upper frames of her glasses. She glanced Sarah's way and smiled at her silence. "Don't be so shocked. I come here all the time."

Sarah knelt by the cardboard box. It contained stacks of records, their sleeves torn or faded or entirely missing, but sheltered from dust in their nook beneath the desk.

"I've got tapes, too, and a cassette player hidden under my bed," she heard Miriam say. "An old handheld radio. Earbuds. But there's no way I could hide an entire record player in my group home, so I took my LPs here. I found the player in this junk room once while I was wandering around."

Sarah sifted through the sleeves that remained intact, scanning their titles. Beethoven. Charlie Parker. Billy Joel. She held the records like they could slice into her bare hands.

When she turned toward Miriam, her mouth slack with words she could not find, she saw laughter in Miriam's eyes. "I sing, too," Miriam added. "The walls here are thick."

Sarah put the records away just as Miriam got the volume working. The needle dipped through the grooves of the disk; soft static padded out from the speakers. Miriam sat on the floor with the back of her head resting against the wall, facing the windows, and patted the spot beside her. Not knowing what else to do, Sarah lowered herself there. Warmth from Miriam's body whispered against Sarah's right side. She shifted away until a foot of empty space lay between them. Then wished she hadn't.

"Listen," Miriam murmured, and the music began to play.

It sounded like wailing. At first Sarah thought it was a voice, yet the keening had something distinctly inhuman about it. The noise chilled her. But then the piano lifted in—gently, tenderly, the sound of light and water—and the instruments wove together like strands of the softest fabric Sarah had never touched. She had never heard anything so haunting.

"What is it?" she breathed into the dusk of the room. "The first thing."

Miriam closed her eyes. "It's an instrument called the theremin. You use it by holding out your hands, like this." She floated her right hand in front of her, shoulder height, and stretched her left one to the side. "You don't press or pluck anything, you just move. The frequency changes depending on where your hand interferes with the vibrations. Kind of sounds like singing, right?"

Sarah studied Miriam's reaching hands, her still-closed eyelids. She wanted, at that moment, to put her mouth to Miriam's throat and taste the texture of her lovely, ragged voice. But she pushed the thought away. The theremin filled up all the space in the room, turned the air thin and fragile. The only instrument played by not being touched.

Then Sarah stared out the windows. It was already dark; it was December, the month Miriam was born. She had just turned seventeen. The two of them sat like that for a long time, conscious only of their breathing, of the music, of each other, and not of the classes expecting their return. The darkness seemed to swallow everything but this little room. They listened until the needle slipped into the center of the disk and the otherworldly song slipped, in turn, into silence.

Miriam opened her eyes. Sarah saw tears there, just bordering her lower lash line, the second before Miriam blinked them away and smiled again. She held up the record sleeve. "See this?"

The cover showed a woman poised over a bizarre box that had an antenna jutting out of it, her hands positioned just as Miriam had demonstrated. "That's Clara Rockmore," Miriam told her. "She was the world's best theremin player. I only have this one record of hers, but it's my favorite one I've got."

Something sad and sweet had settled beneath Sarah's skin, and it had reached the deep place she did not like such things to go. "Miriam," she said. "You know you shouldn't be doing this."

"It's beautiful," Miriam said quietly. Her voice turned brittle. "You'll get to listen to whatever you want, all your life. How come I can't listen now?"

Sarah stood. She had lost track of the number of times a fellow student had said that to her, muttered it to their friend, thought it when she passed by: *You'll never lose what I'll lose.* The other children in her group home would not let her forget it, shunned and envied her for this supposed privilege. None of them understood that she thought the same toward them. They did not comprehend, or chose not to comprehend, what she would lose instead, the infinite loneliness of it.

"You're setting yourself up to suffer in the future," she said to Miriam, while her hands, moving of their own accord, formed an unspoken plea: *I'm scared for you.*

"I'd rather lose it and miss it than never know it at all." And Miriam stood too, to flip the record to its next side.

*   *   *

A month before Minori's first visit, Sarah interpreted for a city council candidate's public forum. Few events provide such accommodations, but sometimes Sarah appears in the corner of a television screen anyway, echoing politicians' speeches whenever campaign rallies pass through the city. She knows she has a hiring advantage as someone both hearing and fluent in sign language— and she knows she must save up for the inevitable day her last pension check arrives in the mail.

Sarah stood at the base of the stage of a small auditorium, scanning the rows of seats. Local attendees took turns asking the candidate about his policies. No one in the crowd seemed to be following her, so she slipped into half-mindlessness, allowing her hands to respond without thinking. Then an audience member asked the candidate to describe his stance on government-funded restoration programs.

Sarah began to sign the question before she realized what it asked. Until then, she had never heard the mention of extractions while working an event. She suspects that debate moderators never raise the issue for the same reason that Rock Creek Academy lies miles along a barely visited walking trail in preserved public parkland, the same reason that all the group homes likewise skulk deep within the recesses of the surrounding wood. Everything safely tucked away beyond the scope of the city, linked by a bus route that never breaks the treeline. Sarah reads the quarterly reports Rock Creek makes public on account of its state funding. But the program is rarely spoken of—except, she imagines, in elite circles where wealthy families whisper referrals to each other when a child is born deaf or blind or some other way deemed wrong.

So Sarah's hands stumbled into stillness halfway through the question.

But the candidate strode smoothly into his answer. "The way I see it," he said, "the restoration academies function like any other government welfare program. They serve the people. They provide jobs—teachers, bus drivers, surgeons. They restore the disabled. When a family cannot support a child, they have an option other than that of sinking deeper into poverty, or resorting to an illegal abortion."

Sarah once told Miriam that she liked that Rock Creek was a girls' school. "They're all girls' schools," Miriam said. She explained that the success rate of extractions was much higher for girls than for boys, so restoration programs stopped admitting male newborns. Removing senses from young women proved more cost effective, the reports indicated; it was just easier to take from their bodies.

"Restoration works just like anything else," the candidate explained. His voice rang clear and resonant; his suit fit him perfectly. "An exchange of assets. Everyone involved gives something and receives something in turn. And society benefits."

Sarah watched her gloved hands work, watched them give shape to his words and send them out into air. There was nothing else she could have done.

*   *   *

A hitch in Minori's breath—and Sarah realizes she has lingered too long in her memories. She wrenches out of them like a needle jumping a scratch.

Minori's lips are slightly parted, her eyes riveted on the television. On its screen, two people press their faces against each other. Their arms encircle each other's bodies, grasp each other's clothes, cling with a delicate ferocity.

Sarah snatches the remote and turns off the television.

Minori sits frozen on the couch. The black screen reflects her glassy expression, as if the scene of the two figures still swims behind her eyes. That is something Sarah has never had, will never have. Perhaps she could have, perhaps she almost did—but it's too late now. She can tell Minori knows she will never have it either.

Minori moves one palm toward the place the remote had been, pauses when she realizes it's in Sarah's grasp. "Oh," she says. "I didn't know…" Her eyes are still unfocused. "You don't have to turn it—"

"Let's do something else," Sarah says. Minori brings her hands back into her lap, twisting them around one another. Without knowing it, Sarah does the same. All she had wanted was to keep Minori's mind off her extraction, to do anything but remind her of what the surgeon would take from her tomorrow. To give her a good memory to hold onto. This visit was meant to be different from all her prior visits, in that way.

For Minori's last lesson, just a week ago, Sarah took her back into the city. She led her not to a store but to the tallest hotel building for blocks. Sarah knew it well.

She showed Minori inside the great glass elevator that slid all the way up and down the building's central axis. Sarah pressed the button for the top floor. Minori stood beside her, straight-kneed and bewildered, as they watched the figures below grow smaller and smaller through the clear walls.

When they reached the top, Sarah pushed the button for the bottom floor, and again the many levels of elevator machinery and shuffling people slipped past them.

They went up again.

They repeated this for nearly an hour. Minori said nothing, just tilted her head to appraise the assortment of people that entered or exited the elevator on the stops between. She swayed a little, absorbed in quiet contemplation. Finally she turned her face toward Sarah in a question that did not need to be spoken to be understood.

Again Sarah touched her finger to the first-floor button and watched it light up without sensing the pressure. "This is what it feels like," she said.

"What do you mean?"

The constant weightlessness. The uncanny emptiness. The awareness of being, of moving, but never anchoring to any one thing: perpetually liminal, forever untethered.

Instead of answering, Sarah stepped off at the ground floor. When Minori made to follow her, she held out a hand—didn't make contact, just blocked the girl's way. "It's your turn," she said.

Minori gazed up at her. For a moment, Sarah saw something in her expression—an incredulous tensing of her mouth which seemed so familiar—that made her wonder whether Minori would stride past her and out the hotel. But then it disappeared. Maybe she had only imagined it.

Instead, Minori edged back into the elevator. The image burned in Sarah's mind all week: Minori's thin shoulders trembling even as she lifted her chin in a show of determination, all by herself in that huge, sleek box. Minori pressed the button. And the machine lifted her up, farther and farther from where Sarah stood watching in the middle of the lobby, until all she could see of Minori was the shiny black strip of her hair.

She descended and, with one hesitant glance at Sarah, rose yet again. Minori glided past other people, could see them and nothing more, separated as she was by the thin glass that rendered them both visible and impossible to reach. Sometimes she looked down at Sarah, locked in place on the other side of a window.

Sarah was still not sure why she had spent so much time riding that elevator after her own extraction. But she could think of no better way to explain what would happen to Minori.

After another hour, she waved the girl over to her. She saw Minori step off the elevator, unsteady, as if doubting the solidity of the floor, weariness slouching her spine, and knew that she understood.

She sees the same dread now, the same tiredness, as Minori sits in her living room and stares at nothing. "What else do you want to do?" Sarah urges her. Minori does not answer.

Sarah will be with her in the extraction clinic tomorrow, will continue to receive her once a week afterward. But really it is something Minori will go through alone.

*   *   *

Silence came for Miriam in January. The class was in the middle of a vocabulary lesson, headphones on—Sarah included—signing words back at the teacher. Then the door opened and a woman on administrative staff showed Miss April a sheet of paper. Miss April signed, *Miriam. Go.*

Sarah first thought of the record player, of the cassettes under Miriam's bed. But Miriam rose coolly from her seat and followed the administrator out the classroom without a single glance back.

She did not return to class. She did not stop by the library, either. Sarah waited for her for the full hour, ignoring her homework and the steadily strengthening thrum of her heart. When it came time for her math class, she left the library and headed for Miriam's secret room instead.

Miriam had taken her there a couple more times since the first; Sarah found it after a few wrong turns. No music played behind the door. She wrapped her hand around the doorknob as she peered over her shoulder into the empty hall. Unease pulsed in her fingertips. She opened the door.

Miriam was inside, not sitting on the floor or rooting through boxes but leaning against the window, staring out into the campus. She turned and looked at Sarah blankly, as though she had never seen her before. Sarah shut the door behind her.

"Miriam." It was all she ever seemed able to say.

Something sharp replaced the blankness in Miriam's eyes; she lifted one shoulder and one corner of her mouth. "It was going to happen eventually."

Through the window, the sun sunk below the trees of the wood. Sarah listened to the sound of her own breathing.

"You know"—Miriam removed her glasses, held them up to the dim lights—"when I was born my parents chose for me to have my sight extracted. But then I developed astigmatism as a kid.

So the program switched me to different classes, switched me to a different home. I think that maybe that's why I've never been able to get used to it. For years I thought they were going to take my eyesight, not my—"

She stopped. Miriam turned her face away and put her glasses back on. "I'll still get to see, though. Isn't that nice? I can look out as many windows as I want."

She fell silent after that. The two of them stood in a room of broken and unwanted things.

"When?" Sarah asked.

"One week." Miriam tried to grin, but the line of her mouth trembled, and then broke. The tears came. They spilled out this time, rapidly and yet noiselessly, as if sound was already lost to them. Her shoulders flinched. Her eyes roved around the room, searching for someone to help her, but there was only Sarah standing stiffly in the center, watching Miriam cry.

Miriam's hands twitched at her sides. The palms turned upward and then over again, flinging away from her body: *I don't want to. I don't want to. It's not fair.*

She had always seemed so brave to Sarah, so unconcerned. In the midst of her horror Sarah understood, now, the too-bright laughter, the collected stories about past students, the extensive, memorized extraction facts. She lifted her hands so Miriam could see them, signing, *I know. I know.*

Miriam paused. Her throat rattled. Her wet eyes met Sarah's, stretched with terror, a prey animal's, and Sarah did not understand what was happening until Miriam's hands were nearly upon her own. One moved forward and the other extended to the side, not to play an instrument but to enact something unspeakable—greedy and ready to grasp, to clutch close, to hold on.

Sarah stepped back just in time.

Miriam's arms froze. She slowly drew them back into herself. And of all the things Sarah wishes she could forget—the school, the group home, the sight of the surgeon leaning over the darkening borders of her vision—she wishes she could forget Miriam's expression the most. Her brows just barely lifted in surprise, the tears still smeared on the tip of her nose. The recognition of betrayal already cooling her wide eyes.

Sarah opened her mouth, but Miriam moved past her and out the door before she could speak. She had no idea what she would have said, anyways. Maybe: *I'm sorry.* Maybe: *I know you weren't trying to hurt me.* Maybe: *You have already ruined yourself. I cannot let you ruin me too.*

That was the last time she saw Miriam. She did not return to school for the rest of the week; she never had an official last day. Sarah sat in sign language class with an empty seat beside her. She often wondered how Miriam passed the time not spent in school. Maybe she had faked an illness, and lay in bed listening to all the songs she could while she still had the chance. Or maybe she had burned every last cassette in preparation for the silence ahead.

Sometimes Sarah left the library just to return to the room and play a record alone. One day she found the door locked, and it stayed that way. She sat by herself on the bus. She kept practicing sign language and lying awake at night, waiting for the day an administrator would summon her to the school office and give her a sheet of paper with a date written on it. She did not have to wait very long.

*   *   *

"Minori," Sarah says. "Let me show you something."

Minori is still someplace far away. She lifts her head, though, as Sarah crosses the room and crouches by the record sleeves the girl had examined earlier. Sarah selects a disk and places it beneath the needle. "I think you'll like this. Listen."

The record waltzes, and a strand of sound wobbles out. It is so thin, so tenuous; the thread of it traces sweeping patterns in the air between them. Then the pitch becomes sonorous, full-throated. Sarah imagines it reverberating inside the hollowness of her body. It is so light and so heavy all at once: the most mournful melody in the world.

Minori tips one ear toward the sound. She scoots closer to the armchair where Sarah returns to sit. "What is it?"

"Theremin."

"It sounds sad." The vibration dips and swivels. "This is what all your records are?"

"Some of them," says Sarah. "I just like to collect the albums of this particular artist." She tries to recall what it felt like to sit next to Miriam in that little dark room. She cannot tell whether she truly remembers the warmth or only remembers the fact of there having been warmth.

Minori lays her head on the couch's arm. "Can I sleep here?"

Sarah nods, and Minori bundles the tattered throw blanket around her. The top of her face peeks out from the covers, framed by the collar of her coat. "Don't let me oversleep."

She is worried about missing her appointment. For whose sake? Surely Minori would not mind passing tomorrow morning under the safety of her blanket, waking in the evening as if her scheduled extraction had been nothing but a nightmare.

Then Sarah understands: She is the one Minori does not want to disappoint. The thought sends a blurry sense of horror echoing through her until she takes a deep breath to muffle the sound of it. Her throat tightens; she is aware of the way her breath struggles through. "I won't."

"Good." Minori's eyelids are half-closed. "Promise you'll be there when I wake up? After tomorrow, I mean."

"I promise."

No one waited beside Sarah's bed when she woke up. That was, more than anything, why she finally agreed to host a touch extraction student once a week. That, and the last thing the Rock Creek recruiter had told her before she left.

"All I ask is that you consider it," the woman said when Sarah returned from the kitchen. "The girl is living in a group home for taste-smell students right now. She's fourteen."

"Too early," Sarah snapped. The thought of another child slated for touch extraction disgusted her.

"Her name is Minori May," the woman added.

And Sarah was back at the library, waiting for Miriam to cut class and find her and tell her a story in that wonderful, scraping voice.

Minori. Miriam. The names blended together in her head. She could never save either of them.

Minori's soft breathing mingles with the lilting theremin until the first side plays out. Sarah rises to flip the disk. Her gloves are usually a bit dirty by the end of the day; not wanting to tarnish the record, she slides them off and leaves them neatly folded over the arm of her chair. As she repositions the needle, Minori's voice startles her.

"I don't want to go back to my group home tomorrow."

"I know," Sarah murmurs. "I know."

The girl's body forms a barely perceptible mound on the couch, and still she can see the trembling beneath the blanket. "Sarah," Minori whispers, "I'm so scared."

Sarah presses play. The song unwinds like a memory. She sits in her chair and lets the numbness inside her create a feeling of its own, something yawning and unutterably deep.

She thinks of the branch of the honey locust tree that always tapped on the other side of her window. What would have happened if she had reached out and grabbed it, wrapped her fingers around the thorns until they punctured flesh, hooked into veins, rent ribbons of red that turned her nerves to fire? It would have hurt so much. It may have been worth it.

*   *   *

Tomorrow, Sarah will sit beside Minori in the school van on the way to the extraction clinic. Sarah will still be sitting beside her when she wakes from the procedure. First Minori will vomit into a plastic bag, a reaction to the anesthesia. She will drop the plastic bag because she will not know how to hold it. Vomit will leak across the floor. There will come the realization, and the horror of realization. There will be a long, terrible silence.

But tonight, Minori sleeps quietly on the couch. Sarah sits beside her even now, watching her rest. She sees Minori's eyelids barely lift, thin white crescents peering beneath, and the little, ungloved hand reach out from under the blanket. She does not feel the little hand wrap around her own, but she sees it happen. And she lets it stay there.

Minori's eyes finally close. Clara Rockmore plays on.

__DANIELLE SHERMAN__ is a first-year MFA student at the University of British Columbia in Vancouver. Her work has appeared in or been recognized by the North American Review, *the* Los Angeles Review, *and* After Happy Hour, *among other publications. She is the recent recipient of the Sudler Prize for undergraduate artists, the Artistine Mann Award in creative nonfiction, and the Grace Abernethy Scholarship in cross-genre writing. She serves as the Associate Producer of the 2026 Brave New Play Rites Festival and as a prose reader for* The Adroit Journal.

Not Deer

Sena Moon

A scar seared the nape of your neck in welts of buttermilk and apricot. Baby lightning. Pie crust. I gasped how that must have hurt; *You're so brave, and like, so pretty.* The praises were met with wide-eyed horror, and you didn't speak to me for months.

We were classmates in second grade, again at fourth. By then, you were less of a riddle. Jamie L. Peony was simply the girl who was sick all the time. Your name made waves in local news with family portraits sunny and airbrushed. Two siblings flanked you in the frame, a brother and a sister who were sickly *but thankfully not on her level.*

"Are you talking about Jamie?"

Two faces swerved as one. Those days, my parents were glued to the love seat, heads abutted like flowers drinking in the sun. Common subjects of discussion: the internet, that isolated freckle on Mom's eyelid, and Dad's chronic but improving conditions.

"No," Mom lied.

"Don't eavesdrop. It's very rude," Dad admonished.

I personally thought adults should mind mouths around open ears, that my parents were being unfair. But Dad steamed squishy songpyeons, and Mom swum laps with me at the neighborhood pool, so forgiveness came easy. Like my Grandma Arabella—or MaBella—once said, moss to a rock.

*   *   *

At the same time, I had to dig deep to forgive Mom for calling your mother *stunning*. When hyperboles leapt from my mouth like *I'm dying of hunger* or *My head will explode from decimals*, Mom called me out. "That counts as a lie, and God knows it." But then she'd say, "You look stunning in that dress, Barb." She didn't, and God knows it.

Mrs. Barbara Peony (née Paden), your mother, liked to wreath herself in floral dresses, with a cinch clip to rival a championship belt. Your house reeked of Aqua Net, of heart-shaped potpourri in carmine red and bubblegum pink. In this Hallmark Valentine scene, she sat like a buttercream cake, smiling her juicy smiles at you—just you.

"I'm kind of scared of your mom," I once confessed.

Do you recall the summer before fourth? The pool offered cherry popsicles. We were barely acquainted, but you turned to me with clear eyes, stained lips. Oaks that bordered the gazebo threw a glossy sheen over our bodies, speckling light on skin as a cicada fell from their porous canopy—just the husk.

"Don't say that."

"Sorry for being rude," I added. "Dad says I can be very rude."

*   *   *

Some nights, Mom sighed, "That poor girl," and I immediately knew.

"Is she okay?"

"She's very sick."

"Like how much? More than Uncle Thomas?" Because he was arguably the sickest person I knew. Uncle Thomas took a handful of pills every morning, and then again throughout the day. He joked that others walked dogs but he walked his oxygen tank, Gertie G the Third, honk if you know my bird.

"Your uncle is not named Thomas."

"He looks like Thomas the Tank Engine."

She lowered her book. "You can't measure sickness like that."

Afterwards, Mom would pretend to read. But her mind was occupied with *poor, dear Jamie*, the way moms cried for every sick child in the world.

Let's be frank. Nothing about you screamed poor. Dear maybe, since Make-A-Wish had your wish made true. Your family went on sponsored trips, scoring Disney parades and official merch at Universal. At playdates, you recounted wonders like the sensational taste of the Unbirthday Cake from *Alice in Wonderland*—which wasn't like how you'd imagined, nothing "un" about it. Must be the lack of wishes, I'd nod sagely before returning to ribosome, chloroplast, and cytoplasm.

By then, we were fourth graders. Assigned seating had worked its magic, and we were inseparable. But our friendship was carefully monitored, for this ship had caveats. Playdates were held at the Peony residence since most houses didn't have the accommodations necessary to cater to a fragility of Jamie's *caliber*. You and I learned to tune out when, for the sixth time that month, your mother outlined the heart-stopping tale of how her baby braved a Chiari decompression surgery, and so soon after her heart palpitation scare! My baby reassured me, groggy as she was from all that medication. *What do you make of that, Hannah?* She wouldn't set down the cupcakes until I wowed.

To us, school was the land of the free. We exchanged outrageous illustrations of teachers and opined on the recent craze over butterfly clips—cute, but tacky. We marched to classes hand in hand and concocted games of our own.

"Fact or fiction? Butterfly clips are cute if used responsibly."

"Fact, but define responsibly."

Fact or Fiction was one we played often. The rules were simple. One person pitched a scenario that straddled the line between fact and fiction while the other assessed its verisimilitude. But unlike the school-mandated version, our game had naught to do with getting facts in order. The experience of watching *The X-Files* felt very real but not the memories of a potential thermonuclear war nor the latent epidemic of prescription opioids. What was fact to us may have been fiction to others. A distinct line bisected insiders and outsiders, for the crux of the game lay in truth mongering, in embracing the other's reality as a certain kind of truth.

"Fact or fiction? I'm *such a retard* for reading during break."

"Fiction. Nina says that because she can't read."

"True."

"Fact or fiction? My doctor says I'm due for another checkup."

"Fiction. Doesn't sound like your doctor."

When classmates made fun of my eyes, you affirmed their cruelty. When you deemed your mother a monster, I validated your horror. We never gave our demons, however small, the benefit of the doubt because this ship sailed free—in tandem. And how we relished the open sea. Cue the bathroom on the second floor of the library. Away from Mrs. Peony's beady blue watch, we smiled before the looking glass, cheeks puffing like cupcakes rising in the oven. In our hands, my entire stash of chocolates, wafers, and toffee galore.

Before sampling the peanut butter cups, I remembered to ask, "Aren't you allergic to nuts?" Because someone like Aimee J. might die ingesting anything nuts.

"I'm not sure."

"How can you be not sure? Maybe we shouldn't."

At this, you slipped the whole disk into your mouth tongue-first, never removing your eyes from mine. *Fiction.*

*　*　*

There and then, my understanding of the universe expanded. It now included the concept of X, far before the curriculum touched algebra. You, my independent variable.

That year, MaBella mailed cash and a giant box of Hawaiian macadamia chocolates for my birthday. The weeks leading up, you and I had made up for lost time with maple nuts and peanut brittle, pecan tarts oozing dark treacle. Anything in the cupboard really, until Mom started regulating my sugar intake.

I meant to take the whole box, but Mom stomped her foot down.

"Just, two."

"I'm going to share!"

Dad slipped an extra into my hands before fixing the TV channel on *M*A*S*H*. The precious nuggets were wrapped in cellophane and sealed, with a Care Bear sticker because you were partial to Care Bears.

But the following morning, a rap on the door shattered our morning lull.

"Jamie? Your mother's here."

We hadn't even begun roll call. The room hushed as you gathered your belongings, the chocolates returned. Later, we heard through the grapevine that you were sick again, that an elongated stay was imperative to handle an illness of this caliber. I had to look up that aggravating word, caliber. You were to undergo another surgery in May, and so soon after the fucking Chiari.

*   *   *

As MaBella once said, bad things arrived in threes. True to her words, Father lost his job after you left. Mom grew lax about my sugar intake, and candy staled in your absence, its sickly sweet heralding a long and dreary winter.

Life grew, slippery. A presentation on Vasco da Gama was hardly a priority when I'd lost faith in a universal reality. Astonishingly, our peers accepted the world as presented, like it was their prerogative. To them, Hannah Choi was sensitive and Mrs. Peony a tortured saint. Ashley suspected I'd grown a brain worm. *Nobody play with Hannah unless you wanna get infected.*

As spooky ghosts gave way to anthropomorphized turkeys as the dominant theme downtown, I frequented pharmacies after school, wandering the aisles for a panacea. Uncle Thomas took prednisone for inflammations and Tenormin for blood pressure, but neither were available over the counter. He wondered why on Earth I'd like to know. *Homework?* No, this inquisitive mind stemmed from a selfish place. If I could alleviate one of your symptoms, would you return to me?

Every bottle came with its own cautionary tale, such as side effects and consequences of excessive dosage. My research uncovered a nauseating truth. The leaflets affirmed that fixing individual symptoms didn't cut it, for the end-all of treatments was the elimination of the primary cause. So how ironic it was that I ran into yours at a pharmacy.

"Just had an amazing session with Dr. K. We're close to nailing what's been ailing Jamie this year. Kills me to specify year because life hasn't been kind to me and my babies. Like our engine dying last week—just worst timing. But I'm a believer and my baby's a trooper."

The voice rose above the carols, stopping me short by the vitamin bottles.

"The Y clinic was pivotal in sussing out her primary allergens, but we failed to identify what was triggering those migraines. After a flipping year!"

A gap between C and K revealed the ungodly tableau: white flowers molding the sweater dress down to the stockings; a back cinched by a clip holding all that wanted to come loose; Mrs. Barbara Peony cruising aisle eleven, her phone snug in her palm like a pocket pistol.

"Listen, I'm talking commitment. If our doctor is not with us a hundred percent, what's the point? She asked me to rethink the treatment plan because it might be, quote, too much. Rethink *my* commitment to *my* child? The gall."

She flexed her free hand, the tips pointed ballerina pink.

"When it's your kid, you need your healthcare advisor to be hands on, bit nosy. V was a valid entry point, but we were ready for the upgrade."

Her lips puckered before splitting happy.

"Yes, thank you most for the reminder. The engine died last week, and there's no way we can coordinate the hospital visits with three sick kids. We *do* prefer cash but anything helps.

"What about a video to kickstart the drive? Chris is all about home videos, and recent ones have been hospital this and treatment that. They're a powerful archive of our healing journey. Yes, post-op ones too. Mm, I know, just breaks your heart.

"Our prime suspect is her heart, but these doctors are so squeamish about open-heart surgery. Mmhm, absolutely.

God has a plan, and I'm just a follower. We're aiming for April, but it's up in the air."

I glanced upwards.

"I know, she's the neck that turns my head. I always tell her, Mommy loves you. You're a right doll for manning the drive. Appreciate you. Tell Shay I said hi."

And I was off.

The next few hours were admittedly hazy. But I'm positive you came to the door alone. I was gasping from the run, a little dazed, face pinkish. My words tumbled out unplanned: *Come with me, tonight. MaBella will let you stay until we're old enough to sow untamed oats. I've some money saved, nearly seventy dollars.*

You looked confused, so I had to explain. She wants to open your heart. Your neck and now your heart; some things must remain closed.

That night, you shimmied down the drainpipe like an 80s delinquent. I had a backpack and a plan. We'd grab Amtrak tickets and call upon arrival because my parents were cool, but not that cool. But listen, MaBella, she makes raspberry cobblers out of this world. She has two cats, the Baron and Lady Beatrice, both cheesy males. Her house is filled with unattractive but interesting trinkets that she always lets you play with. And she never says no to a bedtime story.

The evening had the echoes of a summer past. We rode a trail that split into a fork, the right of which sloped into the main road. From there, the station was a stone's throw away.

You were surprisingly agile. We half-walked, half-sprinted, keeping pace with the clouds. I lagged, but you were glowing, the evening stars in your eyes.

"I was almost a cheerleader."

"For real?"

"Yeah, I'm really good."

You spun a cartwheel to prove your point, and I had to agree. Really good. Maybe cheerleader-level good.

"You should have been a cheerleader at Groff's!"

Our school colors would have gone fabulously with her strawberry blonde curls. Then, I realized the sad truth. Without the veil of Mrs. Peony, you would have had many friends.

"I'm kinda bad at sports."

"But you're a really good coordinator."

"What does that mean?"

"Planning. Organizing and planning stuff." You waved your hands in simulacrum of work.

This pleased me to no end. My dream was to be a pastry chef, but that wasn't the point. Looking back was an oxymoron. We were always marching forward, even as we turned our heads. What we saw in our wake was not the past but a glimpse of who we might become.

"What was that?"

We paused, mid-conversation. For the first time in an hour, our ears perked to the night, bush crickets staging mating calls as our flashlight zigged, dogwoods to poplar to moss.

"There's something following us."

Fear caught up so quick, I stuttered. "A person?"

You fumbled with the light. A click and instantly, everything was more sound than shape. Our eyes adjusted as the footsteps crunched louder, slim haunches parting the bushes, limbs distending beyond our usual comprehension. A red mouth opened and closed in mimicry of speech. I screamed and screamed at the impossible sight.

"Han. Hannah."

A gentle shake.

"Han, it's gone. You're okay." You assumed such an adult tone that self-awareness washed like rain. I started sobbing. How could I have been so naive? Whatever my intentions had been, you knew it to be a temporary Band-Aid, another wish made true.

"I'm so sorry."

"What for?"

You wanted to see the Baron and Lady Beatrice. Two scoops of jammy cobbler, and then a bedtime story. You were right excited for one.

"Let's keep going?"

How small we compared to the stars. Our backpacks weighed heavy, and our feet blistered. There was thirty more minutes of hiking to do. With no felines nor cobblers on me, out came something tried and true:

"Fact or fiction? What my dad saw was a deer."

Continuing our trek, I launched into an anecdote kept unspoken, unvoiced.

It was winter, and Mom had sold her car. We piled up in a run-down Ford F-150 that MaBella was kind enough to rent us. Up front, the road was a vanishing point. To the back, it faded pitch black. Snow started to fall, soft and bone-white against the cracked windshield. The radio was off or perhaps broken, and Dad hadn't spoken all week. Our headlights paled against the storm, tiny flames caught in a polar vortex.

Suddenly, Dad swerved into the parking lot of a closed Walmart. With our car straddling multiple lines, he went stationary. Mom roused. *Dae, what's wrong?*

"It's nothing."

"Are we out of gas?"

"There was a deer," with such a faraway look that Mom turned to check up on me. I pretended to be asleep.

"Roadkill?"

"No, a live one. Huge buck. We missed it by an inch. It was on my side of the road, and I only saw it as we passed. Just the silhouette. If I'd gone any slower or it had stepped forward, our car would have been totaled."

Mom chewed on this awhile.

"Okay, then thank God we didn't hit it."

"It's the other way around. It decided for us."

"I can drive the rest of the way."

"I swear."

The door opened to a flurry of white. Dad slipped into the passenger seat as Mom slipped on her driving gloves. Dad had never driven in snow before coming to the States and falling in love with a math teacher. Even now, he had trouble reading English. He still insisted driving every road trip, at least eighty percent of the way.

"Just a close call," Mom said of that night and every night that befell us.

We had inched across the interstate with our eyes peeled, for the darkness required the best of our attentions. Not unlike learning to accept the night, that we were small and pointless, navigating an angry, barren sea.

When I finished my tale, you nodded.

"Bet it was a not deer."

You proceeded to educate me on the *not deer*, of a creature so resembling deer that witnesses assumed they'd had a brush with the familiar creature. But deer it was not.

I drew breath and tasted gnats.

"What's the point of telling them apart? Does it matter if what we saw was a deer or, whatever this Not Deer is?"

Because either way, we'd had a brush with death.

"It matters when no one believes you."

And loneliness swelled like a flaccid balloon.

Once the heat returned and our bills were paid, Dad told Mom, "You're right. It was a deer." The flickering light meant the three-way bulb we bought from Kroger was a lemon, not the conduit of a spiritual presence. Uncle Thomas, no, Theodore must have fallen ill due to his years working at the paper mill, from dust exposure and a genetic propensity for cancer. It's not because, as Great Aunt Sophie claims, he ran over a pregnant doe in the midst of spring. Dad getting laid off had nothing to do with his funny-sounding name—Dae-young. People genuinely forgot that his English name was David—not Danny boy, Daniel, or much later, Dae Kim.

At the time Dad immigrated to the US, the buzzword was melting pot. He imagined a fondue with forty different kinds of cheese, pungently delightful and soft to the touch. Later, he revised the analogy to hot pot. We're thrown into the boil, but certain areas are sectioned off, and individual ingredients are involved. Dad considers himself a bok choy. *Get it? Choi? Haha.*

He fell out of religion during the 70s but still prayed, like a starving teen sneaking snack cakes after midnight. I'd seen black-and-white photos of him looking exceptionally foreign, with graffiti framing the M1 helmets. He was a shade thinner, taller, with a bronzed smile befitting a country fast emerging from poverty.

But by the time I came in the picture, Choi Dae-young was a changed man. He sentenced himself to repentance hoping for eventual parole, but every bump on the road was reason to resist. According to Mom, happiness was a straight path—straight as an arrow—and a person needn't be anything but a bow. Dad believed repentance took shape in misery. Storms sent him into small spaces. He loved sun showers but hated the sound of rumbling thunder. Mom had full control of the quilts and the comforters because Dad stained them, especially around his legs. I bought cotton pajamas on his birthday, in all colors and patterns because they never lasted.

Dad's stories had a mythical quality in that fiction belied facts. Sometimes, he only shot at the ground and the skies, never at lives. Other times, a grenade wiped out a bunker that held not only soldiers but civilians. Children. He'd swear he did not know. How could he have known?

When I explained Fact or Fiction over dinner, Dad had made an ugly face. He retreated to his study and brooded for days. At family trips, he cracked jokes nonstop, making fun of hikers, the mountaineers' creed, and Mom's zeal for life with self-flagellating cynicism. I used to think he suffered from a poor taste in jokes, an affliction that plagued dads all over the world. But his edges were jagged with resentment, and Mom felt pierced. Why couldn't they enjoy life for what it was? *For once, talk to me.*

For all it was worth, it was a deer.

Yet I still offered you in that forest, "Tell me what you saw. Then I'll tell you what I saw."

But before we could entertain our binaries, a crunch brought us back. The creature without a name returned with an agenda and eyes that were all pupil, no whites. They began spinning like a whirligig. You and I backed into an oak, counting white spots multiplying on a mottled back. Eight, thirteen, twenty-one.

"Are you seeing what I'm seeing?"

Someone was crying. It was hard to put to words.

The creature's mouth widened, bevel teeth heralding death by a thousand cuts, the hands of a sick mother, or residual symptoms of war. Human lips declared we'd never grow old. Not unless you choose to, but why would you choose to, when life was a slow, painful journey to the end? Think about that. No, don't think. You're not pretty when you think.

I sniffled, *My name is Hana, not pretty.* It meant *one* in Korean or *God's grace* in English. God was hana-nim in Korean. It worked on many levels.

"That's kind of pretty," you said appreciatively. "How come you never said?"

The creature ignored our banter. It clicked its hooves and quivered a fleshy smile before splitting open, shuddering red upon red. The head fanfared into a bloom like a garden onto itself, a bowl of teeth and coral charms—such brilliant peonies. Spittle dripped from its cavity, tracing the mandible with loving grace. *Here they come, paper cuts.* We were holding hands when it swallowed us whole.

In the belly of the beast, I accepted the truth.

"You were right. Definitely a not deer."

Dust settles like dew, sieving the last rays of the sun.

*   *   *

Unfortunately, I don't have pictures of Jamie. Back then, Polaroids were the rage. We moved a lot. Marie Kondo was a phenomenon for a hot second.

My parents' basement is a strange space to behold. The walls are full of holes. Last fall, the humane trap caught three field mice in a row that could have been the same mouse. Told you so, said Dad—*when does humane anything work?* But he's turned flexitarian and has stopped humming morbid songs from *M*A*S*H*. Here's his album, kinda worn. Here, some candles Mom bought in bulk. At one point, she got sick of living with two human walls and made a memory table for good times past. Her yoga friend had asked, "Oh my god, who died?" There, the love seat. A working elliptical that Dad declared broken. Vintage Polly Pockets. A mannequin head, Sassy Jane, with glued-on lashes that gave my husband a right scare on New Year's. Dust laced with memories, yet not a single archive remains. In debris, I slip into a marsh of my own design.

Peony is a rare name. Has to be. I scan social media like a hawk to make sure. Dad goes fishing to forget; I web surf to reflect. Mom lights candles in all scents and sizes, trying to accept her odd, introverted kin.

At the train station, we were met by two officers, one male and one female. The ticket master alerted our parents, and Jamie was ripped away to a new state, a new school. We weren't allowed to keep touch. I sailed alone, unsure of the sun. Time flies when you're out in the waters. Her voice is one of the last things I remember, but even this fades, a worn tape on its last warbling tune. That's not to say she left nothing behind.

*   *   *

Since Jamie, my present is a spinning dartboard with two options, deer and not deer.

A "rotting corpse smell" plaguing Spring Mill Park—deer. It was an Easter hunt gone wrong. Stank up the whole park for the better part of a month. Easily explained away.

An elementary school teacher falling asleep with a lit cigarette—not deer. The local news was gauche enough to include a picture of his charred mattress with the word *self-immolation*, now students think he's haunting the Inter-culture room. They shudder and dare each other to peek. But I'd sat in that darkened room, hoping to see his ghost.

A seasoned social worker, pitching dog shit across a lawn out of neighborly spite—deer. That pooch was trouble. He nipped at small children, and the owner never picked up after him. The whole neighborhood is working on a petition to get them training, for both human and dog.

The election—not deer.

Years passing like dull weekends—deer.

Dad refusing therapy and pitching a solo reverse-immigration—not deer.

Mom demanding and getting couples therapy—deer.

My brief stint with mindfulness—not deer.

They reconcile when I present my firstborn. Charlie brings permanent ceasefire. I don't question it. We plan a family trip to Jeju Island that falls on his eighth birthday, our first international trip. Coincidentally, the government is paying for it—'bout a tithe, Dad jokes—with the new Korean American VALOR Act that honors veterans who were denied healthcare in the past. Is this a compromise? Or Dad learning he's been boiling too long in the pot, and it's bad form to reuse ingredients? Personally, I've grown cold on both fact and fiction. But commitment is like stars in the sky. What we see is radiance from many years past, lighting up the now.

"Excited to see Gran and Gramps?"

"Why can't we drive?"

"Your dad needs the car for work. We're saving up for the trip, remember?"

Charlie slumps with the tablet, on which Americans in leotards are competing as mighty ninja warriors. Not deer? But he's engrossed. I look away, then look again.

A passenger on the city bus, with a pie crust riding the nape of her neck. Of average sitting height, with an apple-green beanie resting on her tawny head cocked fifteen degrees as if deep in thought. Straight locks, but you can change hair with any old straightener. I stare, very rudely. Beside me, my child asks what we're having for dinner because he's been hungry since twelve, and that's too high a number. The traffic's light, the weather balmy. She gets off at the City Center Circle, circumventing a puddle making broad strokes with her arms, spry enough to launch into a full, adult cartwheel. Charlie says he wants sundubu-jjigae when we arrive, but not too spicy. He'll have exactly two and a half bowls because, decimals. We add soft tofu to the grocery list. The shuttle lurches forward, with the grace of a somnambulant hound.

Have you been thinking about me? I've been thinking about you—deer.

SENA MOON *is a 2024-2026 Stegner Fellow and the recipient of the 2020 PEN/Dau Short Story Prize for Emerging Writers. Her work has appeared in* The Kenyon Review, Guernica, The Southern Review, *and* Boulevard, *among others. She hails from Seoul, South Korea.*

Stargazers

Amy Wilde

The year my mother died, I was working two jobs: a nine-to-five in state government—hourly pay, no paid leave, no healthcare—and a local TV crew gig on the side. The day the call came, a production trip loomed. I can't remember a damn thing about it, except for the smell of the lilies.

I have an image of myself sitting in my small, windowless office that Thursday afternoon, working with the fluorescent light off and one desk lamp on, when my dad phoned to tell me she was in an ambulance. I remember alerting my boss through choked words, rushing home to throw a bag of clothes together, and driving two hours to my hometown. I remember making phone calls: one of my brothers in case he hadn't heard, a friend to cancel that night's plans. I don't know if I listened to music, if there was sun or rain or both, or when my dad called again to tell me she was gone—I must have been driving, but I don't recall pulling over or anything he said.

"I've lost a parent—both, actually—and get it if you need to back out," the crew leader said on a phone call the next day. He needed to know if he should find a stand-in, switch the ticket, make it work. I thought back to the last time we'd had a death in our family. For the first few days, my childhood home would be filled with an ever-moving assembly line of condolence-bearers with casseroles. The day after the service, a hollow silence would settle over the house like a cold blanket. I couldn't bear the thought of leaving my dad alone inside it. If I didn't get paid for the weekend, I'd be too broke to take off work and stay with him a while.

"I'll be there," I said, and repacked my bag.

In my hotel room, a vase of stargazer lilies greeted me with sympathies from the crew. I carried it onto the plane home that Sunday and sobbed into it for the whole flight, looking out the window at the sky, inhaling the flowers' heady, ambrosial scent, trying to grasp just where, exactly, my mother's soul had gone.

She wore gardenia perfume most days; it reminded her of the shrub my brothers gave her one Mother's Day, the blooms of which she'd place in bowls of water around our small cinder block house each spring. When I think of her sitting still, she's usually in that house, grading spelling tests, watching *Magnum, P.I.*, giving me the kind of advice that would gently point me in the right direction and let me figure out the rest myself. Sometimes she's on the porch swing, singing. When I think of her in motion, it's more abstract, synesthetic. I think of her perfume's almost operatic resonance, of her little bowls of creamy white flowers, of that booming choral alto voice unfurling from her lungs. When I think of her like this, she's not in that house; she's everywhere.

Stargazers, something of a next-door neighbor to gardenias from a perfumer's perspective, have their own similarly narcotic, if slightly less robust, fragrance. Both have a constellation of noted enthusiasts: Sigmund Freud, Billie Holiday, and Hattie McDaniel were all partial to gardenias in their day, while Kurt Cobain's favorite flower was the stargazer, which, at his request, surrounded him by the thousands when Nirvana played *Unplugged.* He wanted the set to look like a funeral, he told the production designer, who added black candles to drive home the theme.

At my mother's service, I placed the vase alongside the other bouquets on the altar where I'd ambivalently prayed every Sunday when I was young and where, eventually, my dad would quietly get married again, to a woman he'd meet at his community center's morning coffee klatch for seniors who called themselves "The Energizers." Years later, he would die, too, and a minister would stand behind that altar and read words I'd written but couldn't say out loud.

Two weeks after my father's service, the moon passed through the midday sky in perfect alignment between earth and sun, lingering for just a minute or two for those of us looking up at it from central Texas. For the occasion, I'd dabbed on a sample of a perfume called "Neroli Ad Astra 19.1," meant to smell like neroli and agave flowers somehow grown in a celestial garden. A few yards away on the crowded bridge where I stood, someone quietly played a few Pink Floyd selections: "Brain Damage," "Eclipse." My dad loved that band. When I was little, sometimes he'd play *Dark Side of the Moon* front to back when my mother and I would leave the house for a few hours. Ever a fan of excellent stereo equipment, even on a blue-collar budget, he'd amassed a setup to his liking and would, on occasion, arrange the living room speakers just so, remove their covers, and sit between them at what he considered to be the perfect distance, like the Maxell man letting the sound blow his hair back. I looked up at the sun's corona encircling the moon, wished he were there, and wondered if maybe he was.

The night of the eclipse, I went to an audiophile bar with a custom Klipsch sound system and a drink special inspired in part by Ry Cooder, another of my dad's favorite musicians, though none ranked as high for him as Leonard Cohen did. I raised a glass to him, sitting between the speakers on my own dark side of the moon, drunk more on grief than whiskey or sotol.

A year after that Pink Floyd record came out, a plant breeder in California developed stargazers, adding them to a specific subgroup of lilies known for their pungency. She did this by modifying the typically downcast rubrum lily so it would gaze up at the sun and other stars, evoking a sense of optimism. Sometime later, a cultivar of scentless stargazers briefly hit the market, but nobody wanted those. After my mom's service, years passed and I moved a time zone away to Austin to try on a new kind of life. I met a friend for dinner one night in a home he was house-sitting for the week and took my seat at the table as he pushed a huge stargazer centerpiece out from between us. When the scent hit me, I wasn't there anymore; I was back on that plane, in my window seat from Miami to Tallahassee, trying to locate my mother's soul like a child trying to understand the alphabet. I couldn't eat the meal, and although he kindly moved the vase when I explained myself, I walked around fractured for days. Was her soul just the energy hovering between her actions and emotions back when she was alive? Was it more than that? Was it gone? Had she left seeds of it in her kids, her students, the people who loved her? Where *was* she? Was she anywhere?

Since that night at the dinner table, I've been aware of scent's point-blank ability to knock the wind out of me, or you, or anyone, and it's changed the way I move through the world. Odor molecules—these volatile organic compounds, named such for how ephemeral and utterly natural they are—go where they please, amorphous, similar to sound but lingering without invitation, their echoes filling our lungs, clinging to the insides of our faces. I think about who else is tormented by their own olfactory ghosts, hiding around corners and poking at their vulnerabilities. The widow whose partner made coffee every morning and imbued its scent with their memory. The assault survivor who can't tolerate whiskey on a lover's breath. The veteran who doesn't dare go near diesel fumes. It's why I won't wear fragrance to a funeral—to save those left behind from being haunted in the years ahead.

Lori Aldaheff wears the same fragrance every day. It's the perfume her fourteen-year-old daughter, Alyssa, often wore before she was killed along with 16 fellow students on Valentine's Day 2018 in Parkland, Florida. Alyssa, a student at Marjory Stoneman Douglas High School, was shot ten times through a window as she hid underneath a table in English class. An excerpt from an Associated Press (AP) article the following year reads:

> Every morning, Lori Alhadeff makes breakfast for her two boys, gets dressed and sprays on her daughter's Victoria's Secret perfume.
>
> The scent is part of her armor, propelling her through her whirlwind of a day as she fields hundreds of emails and juggles two phones, a constant reminder of why she ran for and won a seat on the local school board, and started a foundation to make schools safer. Why she called out President Trump in a televised, gut-wrenching tirade.
>
> "I smell Alyssa," Lori Alhadeff says, "so I feel like she's more a part of me."

The Institute for the Study and Treatment of Loss calls traumatic bereavement "the state of having suffered the loss of a loved one when grief or mourning over the death is complicated or overpowered by the traumatic stress brought about by its circumstances." In cases like these, but also throughout any course of mourning, the bereaved may spend the first year or more beset by "sudden temporary upsurges of grief." One moment, we're fine. The next, we're knocked over by a force greater than ourselves, the enormity of loss washing over us again in a wave we didn't see coming.

Sensory cues can trigger a surge and shove us through our window of tolerance to a place where nothing feels safe or correct. Over time, we might choose to repurpose those cues into survival tools that help instead of hurt, serving as a form of exposure therapy: When it works, a fragrance, flavor, or sound we associate with the loved one we've lost can take on new meaning, giving us comfort or urging us onward.

Scientists think scent's pivotal role in the stories we tell about ourselves and one another has to do with the way it tangles itself up in the process of memory formation, traveling via our shortest cranial nerve and bypassing the thalamus, the part of the brain other sensory information has to groan through, delaying the connection. As says science, so say the arts. Andy Warhol was so aware of fragrance's ability to timestamp itself in one's memory that he took to curating something he called a "permanent smell collection," wearing a perfume or cologne for just a few months at a time, then archiving it and only going back for a huff when he wanted to reminisce about a person or place in time. He did this throughout his life with just a few fragrances per year, building a time machine and neatly separating his past into scented chapters. It's likely why, as I've read, someone close to him slipped a bottle of Estée Lauder's "Beautiful" into his coffin to take with him into the ground. *Don't forget me*, they must have been saying. *Keep me with you.*

The New Yorker journalist Rachel Syme writes of spritzing herself, her pillow, and whatever book she's reading with a perfume containing an oud note each night; she does this because oud, in its natural form, is made from the protective secretions of the agarwood tree, and she thinks of it as a kind of armor against the anxious thoughts that taunt her as she tries to fall asleep. Playwright (and friend of Goethe) Friedrich Schiller swore he couldn't write without taking a whiff of the rotting apples he kept in his desk drawer; whether it worked by superstition or, as cultural critic Maria Popova theorizes, getting him high off the ammonia, we may never know, but Beethoven's revolutionary "Ode to Joy," inspired by Schiller's poem, wouldn't exist were it not for that fetid ritual.

In *Braiding Sweetgrass,* scientist Robin Wall Kimmerer recounts how every time she brings a new ethnobotany class to Cranberry Lake Biological Station to dig up spruce roots, history repeats itself as at least one of the students always, *always*, begins to sing. She attributes this to the oxytocin spike the human brain experiences when we spend a few minutes breathing in the scent of *humus*, the organic matter that forms within topsoil as flora and fauna decay inside it. Just as the earth sustained those who came before us, their bodies now sustain it in return, helping it nourish those of us living today even as we actively destroy it. And aboveground, as author Bill Bryson writes in *The Body: A Guide for Occupants*, "Every time you breathe, you exhale some 25 sextillion… molecules of oxygen—so many that within a day's breathing, you will in all likelihood inhale at least one molecule from the breaths of every person who has ever lived. And every person who lives from now until the sun burns out will from time to time breathe in a bit of you. At the atomic level, we are all in a sense eternal."

Trees, to whatever extent trees can understand things, understand this. Some species use chemical senses to detect when neighbors need nutrients, offering up their own supply through interconnected roots, like a sylvan mutual aid network: Give what you can, take what you need, look out for one another. Worlds within worlds take part in this exchange, breathing one another in and out even after we've gone.

When my dad was in the hospital in his final months, he'd introduce me to guests by telling them about my involvement in a local free fridge program—a series of community refrigerators and pantries available 24/7 for free food and basic necessities, no questions asked. I often go on Sundays and leave meals, snacks, water, and self-care kits, sometimes with scented toiletries and vials of fragrance, another small form of nourishment. On his first birthday after his death, I brought a trunkful of foods he loved— fried chicken, pizza, fresh oranges, instant coffee, sweet iced tea, full-sized Snickers bars. Next to those, I left a blank composition book and pack of blue Bic pens, his favorite. Ry Cooder, his guy, once covered the old Blind Willie Johnson song, "Everybody Ought to Treat a Stranger Right," written not long before my dad was born. He tried to live by that. Both my parents did.

"All of us down here are strangers," go the lyrics. "None of us have no home." When I go home for good, whatever that means for my soul, I want my sendoff to involve natural organic reduction or burial, returning to the earth and giving back what I've been given once I'm too dead to stock up a fridge. Keep a toe dipped into the conversation, I suppose, even if the toe has fallen off.

Until then, I'm learning to keep green things alive from up here, looking down, as opposed to the eventual inverse. I'm starting small: herbs, air plants, three-inch pots of ivy. I lean in and inhale their scent each morning as we tend to one another. Mom was far better at helping her elementary school students bloom than she was at any kind of gardening, but I always laughed at the way Dad could walk past a plant, smile in its direction, and coax an explosion of growth. With him there, our humble backyard, which thinly veiled the site of an old city dump filled with washer/dryers, car parts, and trash, somehow stayed lush with dewberries, kumquats, figs, honeysuckle, and scuppernong grapes on the vine. It was a fragrant sanctuary in a place known for the reek of its paper mill, where the chorus of hometown redneck band Lynyrd Skynyrd's song "That Smell" was a punchline all by itself. When my dad's mother died a year after mine, he moved back into the house he'd grown up in, just a few miles away. The day he died in the ICU, I went there and sobbed when I caught a glimpse of his orange tree out front, hanging heavy with bittersweet fruit.

For years, my mother's ashes sat in a cemetery up the street from the school where she taught without my paying them a visit. For all my indelible ties to her, my bottomless love for her, and my daily moments of connection with her, I'd never felt compelled to stop by; I'd just drive past the entrance on my way into or out of town, kiss my fingertips, and touch the car window. I think of her soul—or, at least, the afterimage of it—as a sprawling and ever-present thing too broad to confine, and the idea that we could or should "place grief here"—as if a memorial service or cemetery could contain the sum of any loss, feels incomplete. But it was May 2021, and I was in my hometown on Mother's Day after a sustained period of difficulty and loss the world over. It felt wrong not to go.

On our way back to his house from picking up sandwiches earlier that day, my dad had wound me through the cemetery to show me where she was. He'd stepped out of the car with me still behind the wheel and walked over to her exact resting place to point it out.

"What bad poetry," I'd thought, watching him, already in his eighties, recede toward the place where his ashes would rest one day, too. But this was still some time before his feeding tube, his oxygen line, the endless, endless beeps. This was when he was still walking, still eating, still breathing on his own.

Later that afternoon, visiting her by myself, I didn't bring stargazers or gardenias. I didn't bring anything. I tucked my facemask into my back pocket and sat beneath a canopy of Spanish moss, babbling to the concept of her as I stared at her name embossed on the columbarium. I held out my phone and played her Willie Nelson's easy, ambling cover of "Stardust," recorded when I was a toddler—an off-the-cuff choice that felt right for reasons I couldn't articulate in the moment. I told her about the book I was writing, the person I'd married, the way I'd moved west, what lockdown had been like. I caught her up on family matters, described the dog I'd adopted, told her we were okay. It felt stilted, talking to the air, to someone I'd been having conversations with in my head for years, but I kept on anyway. I told her how grateful I was for what she'd been and done, and how I hoped she'd known and felt these things when she was still alive. I told her I was sorry. That I missed her. That we were taking care of one another in our own broken ways, best we could.

"I think you know already," I said through tears. "Or knew. But, just in case."

I climbed back into the car with an awkward sense of open-endedness and drove to the airport to board my flight back home. Putting on the mask, I caught a deep whiff of earth from the fabric. It came to mind that while I associate gardenias with her life and stargazers with her death, the scent of soil in which both are rooted would now, for me, forever call to mind her memory, and now my father's, too, and maybe someday mine for someone else looking down at the ground or up at the sky with all their little questions.

The scent of *humus*, of connection, of the potential for growth and regrowth. The scent of us, of our exchange, until the sun burns out.

AMY WILDE is a Florida-born, Texas-based writer living in London as she pursues a Writing MA at the Royal College of Art. Her poetry and essays have appeared in Humana Obscura, Amethyst Review, Poets for Science, The Hairpin, *and elsewhere, and her creative nonfiction work was shortlisted by* Ploughshares *for its 2024 Emerging Writer's Contest. She's currently working on a book about intersections of scent, memory, loss, and legacy. Her newsletter,* Brown Paper Packages, *offers shareable pleasures and connective ideas for deeply chaotic times.*

Sermons

Katie Henken Robinson

Pixie showed up on our doorstep one morning in June, looking more like a carnival sideshow act than our new renter. She was tiny and frail, holding a caged parakeet in one hand and a purse as big as her body in the other. Her hair was dyed purple with grey at the roots, and she wore a tie-dye dress plastered with emojis. When she smiled, I counted three missing teeth.

Dad had told me the night before that a new renter was coming, our third in the span of four months. We started renting out my bedroom after Mom and I got into a car accident last winter. I'd walked away unscathed while she was in a coma, hospital-bound for four months now. It became clear once the medical bills started rolling in that if we wanted to keep the house, we were going to have to share it. We'd stripped my bedroom of the accumulated detritus of my youth—tee-ball participation trophies, a blue ribbon from freshman-year spelling bee, movie posters I copped from the local Blockbuster when it finally closed down—and brought it all down to the basement. Free of my personal junk, the room became the sort of place someone might actually want to live.

When I found Pixie at the door, I was convinced she wasn't the new tenant. She didn't exactly fit our usual renter profile. I hoped she was a Jehovah's Witness or confused grandma on the lam. "Can I help you?" I asked.

"Pixie?" My dad came up behind me, reaching his arm past my shoulder to shake her hand. "Come on in! I'm Ray. This is my son, Charlie. So nice to meet you in person."

Pixie hobbled into the living room, the cage jangling. She set the bird on the coffee table and turned on the TV. "Do you have CNN? That's his favorite."

It took me a moment to realize that by *his*, she meant the bird. I glanced at my dad like, *What the hell were you thinking?*

He refused to meet my eyes and said, "Sure, it's channel 100."

The parakeet seemed genuinely riveted by the TV. He was the color and scent of dehydrated piss and had a strangely judgmental facial expression for a bird. It felt like he was waiting to peck our eyes out.

Pixie wandered into the kitchen and flopped down on a chair. "Sorry, he's just so particular. We preach at a local church on weekends, so on Mondays he's always tired and grouchy."

"You preach?" my dad asked.

"Oh, it's mostly Father Skeeter. I fill in the things he can't say." She laughed. "He's a minister. Real popular around here." Pixie nodded her head toward the cage, and my dad and I simultaneously realized that Father Skeeter, the minister, was indeed the bird. I shot my dad a glance again, and this time he met my gaze with a warning glare.

"Well, it's not a *church* church," Pixie explained, as if that cleared anything up at all. "You two can come sometime! Anyone's welcome. He gives a lovely service."

"I gotta get to work," I said.

"Why don't you bring Pixie's bag to the room first?" my dad said.

I remembered then that I hadn't gotten the room ready like I was supposed to. I'd stolen some beers from the fridge the night before and gotten drunk by myself. In the morning, I was too hungover to run through the renter protocol of cleaning the room, changing the sheets, and removing all traces of my existence. I'd told myself I'd do it later, but by the time Pixie arrived, I still hadn't done shit.

Dad handed me Pixie's bag. "Here, take this."

"Take this. Drink from it," Father Skeeter squawked from his cage.

"Jesus Christ," I said, jumping at his voice, a strange combination between screech and whisper.

"Praise to you Lord Jesus Christ," Father Skeeter intoned.

"I didn't know parakeets could talk," my dad said. He looked more amused than disturbed.

"Oh, they can, but most aren't very good at it. Father Skeeter is special. He was chosen by God." Pixie put her face against the cage and cooed.

I carried Pixie's bag down the hallway to what was once my bedroom, and she followed behind.

"Your dad mentioned that your mom is in the hospital," she said. "I asked Father Skeeter to say a prayer for her at this Friday's mass. He's known to be a real miracle worker, you know."

She stepped into the room. I felt my cheeks grow hot when I noticed the crumpled bed sheets, twisted and smelling of beer. I decided I hated her. For being here, for talking about my mom, for believing her bird's prayers meant anything.

"Room's kinda smelly," she said, glancing around with her nose crinkled. "A bit small for four hundred bucks."

I stared at her, unblinking, a game of uncle. Eventually, she turned away.

"That will be all then," she said dismissively. Even though she'd looked away first, I had the sense she'd won.

"Pixie all set up?" Dad asked when I came back to the kitchen.

"Dad," I said, my voice low. "What the fuck."

He shrugged. "She seems nice enough."

"She seems like a *lunatic*. She thinks her bird is a minister, for Christ's sake!"

"Christ has come, Christ has risen," chanted Father Skeeter.

Dad met my eye. For a moment, I glared at him. But then we were laughing so hard tears came out of our eyes. I grabbed my keys off the table, wiping my eyes with the back of my palm.

"Peace be with you," I said on my way out the door, closing it just as Father Skeeter echoed the refrain.

*   *   *

A month back, I'd taken a shit job for shit pay at Beer World, a drive-through liquor store down the street. I'd been planning to go to college, but after the accident, I threw my future plans out the window. When my acceptance letters rolled in, I put them in the trash. Dad told me I was being stupid, that I had to go. But he couldn't hide the bills piling up on the table, the late notices, the hushed phone calls begging the electric company to give him a few more days. Whatever excitement I'd had about college was gone after the accident anyway. I told Dad there was always next year, that I'd work in the meantime, but really, I had no plans of going, now or ever. When I saw a help wanted sign at Beer World, I applied. I liked the idea of hauling boxes around, breaking my body just to feel like I could.

It started getting hot early this year, and Beer World was sweltering, the air heavy and humid. There were two standing fans covered in grease and dust, spitting grime into the air that swirled about when sun streamed through the entryway.

"Fuck this place, man. I would straight-up murder to work somewhere air conditioned." This was Joey-Jim, who worked the Monday shift with me. He stood in front of a fan, sneezing from the dust. He got his name because there was already another Joey. We would've used his last name, but there was another Hernandez, too. So he got stuck with first and middle.

I nodded lethargically. I kept thinking about Pixie, her bird, how much longer my life would be this way. For a while, I'd thought it would all be temporary. That Mom would recover fast, and things would return to normal. I'd had visions of her coming home in time to drop me off at college, and I'd miss her, but it would be the regular sort of missing. Instead, she'd been in a coma for long enough that it was becoming hard to believe she'd come out of it. Two months of finger twitching might be enough for Dad to hang onto, but I'd done enough research to know there were no guarantees it would ever amount to her waking up. We were staring down a lifetime of drowning in bills if we wanted a chance for her to get better. Dad said the money would work itself out. I hadn't inherited his optimism.

"What's up with you today?" Joey-Jim called over to me. "You seem out of it."

"Who knows. Just thinking about how I was supposed to be at college but instead I'm here, fighting off heat stroke for minimum wage."

"Shit. I'm sorry man." He came closer and cupped my elbow with the palm of his hand, a gesture that felt awkward and too intimate. He'd stripped his shirt off and tucked it into his pocket so it stuck out like a dish towel, his chest glistening with sweat. He looked good. We'd hooked up a week ago—when things were real slow and we stole a six pack to drink in the register booth. In the bathroom in the back, he got on his knees while I leaned against the molded sink. Afterward, I went to count the money at the register.

He hoisted himself up onto the counter beside me, his legs swinging by my side, grazing against me. "You ever done that before?"

I glanced at him briefly, trying not to lose my count. "Do what? Get a blowjob?"

"You know what I mean."

I scoffed. It came out meaner than I meant it. "Yeah, I have. Guys, girls. Whatever."

"You just don't strike me as the type."

"I don't consider myself to be any *type*."

He looked a little forlorn, like he was waiting for something more. I continued to count, refusing to meet his eyes, until eventually he hopped down from the counter and walked away.

We never talked about it after that. I was too freaked about someone at work finding out. Our boss didn't exactly strike me as the tolerant type. I wrote it off as a stupid thing I did because I could, maybe because I'd broken up with my girlfriend a couple days before and just wanted to forget all that. But whenever he acted all gentle and kind, I didn't know how to react. I was too worried that tenderness was a trick, the lead-up to a demand of some kind. It seemed easier to keep my distance.

I moved my elbow out of his grasp. "I should go do inventory," I said. An easy excuse to cross the room entirely.

*   *   *

On Mondays after work, I was supposed to go see Mom at the hospital, but today, like usual, I kicked around Beer World for a couple hours instead. I sat on a bench in the alley next to the shop. It had cooled off, and a breeze rolled across my face. Like always, I stared at my phone and drank can after can of Coke from the vending machine, and then I'd go home and tell Dad I'd been at the hospital. He knew I was lying, but he never called me out on it. I couldn't explain why this made me mad, but it did.

I knew I should go see her. The doctors said talking could help, but it seemed fake to me, the kind of thing they say to make you feel useful when really all you can do is sit and wait. I'd gone in the early days, but it had felt like sleepwalking, my body going into autopilot the moment I walked through the hospital doors. And then one day I went with Dad, and while he held her hand and spoke softly to her, I somehow snapped into it, too aware, too awake. It was like I only just realized the woman in that hospital bed was Mom, and she would maybe never wake up. I ran to the bathroom and threw up, then sat on the floor, raking my hands through my hair and trying not to puke again. I hadn't been back since.

The accident had happened in late February, during that stretch when the days were too warm for snow and so it rained instead, and then at night the roads became slick with black ice. Mom and I were driving home from dinner—we'd gone out, the two of us. That night, it was pitch black and beautiful and the tree branches were encircled in ice. One minute we were laughing and the next a deer jumps out into the road and Mom swerves, and there's a truck coming the other way—*boom*. The car on its side, windshield smashed, air bags out—useless. I was standing there, somehow out on the pavement, useless as the air bags. I don't even remember if I was trying to get her out of the car, or if I was just standing there, saving myself. The truck driver got out, and I could hear him shouting at me, but I couldn't answer. I couldn't do anything. In the end, he was the one who pulled her out. I couldn't look him in the face while we waited for the ambulance. I was too ashamed he'd had to do what I should've done.

Somehow, I walked away with barely a scratch. I had an ugly gash on my forehead from a piece of glass, a bruise across my chest where the seatbelt had been. Everything that escaped me had happened to Mom instead. Broken ribs, punctured lung, the head injury she might never recover from.

The renting had been my idea. I wasn't sleeping half the time anyway, and when I did, it was fitful, punctuated with bad dreams. It felt like a waste of a bedroom. I hated to admit it, but I thought maybe sleeping on the floor of Dad's room would help, just to have someone else there. But it turned out I still couldn't sleep.

"Want one?"

I jumped at the sound of Joey-Jim's voice. I hadn't even noticed he'd walked over.

He had a cigarette hanging from his mouth and another between his fingers, held out to me. "Sorry. Didn't mean to scare you."

"I was just zoning out. Didn't hear you coming over."

He handed me the cigarette and a lighter. I stared at the building next door, a Mexican grocer that was tagged with bubble graffiti that read "Uglee Boy."

"I'm not going to college either," Joey-Jim said.

"Huh?"

"You were talking earlier about not being able to go. I just wanted you to know I get it."

"Oh. Thanks."

"I'm saving up money to apply in a couple years, taking classes at community college in the meantime. What about you?"

"Can we just stop talking about it?"

A look of hurt passed across his face, but then it was gone. He dropped his cigarette and ground it into the asphalt with the toe of his shoe. "All right," he said.

"Sorry. I'm just—"

"No, it's cool. I get it." He stood and brushed off his pants, gave me a soft smile. "I'll see you later."

Somewhere nearby, I could hear kids laughing in the park. A hazy summer glow rippled over everything. I finished my cigarette, then sat there for another hour, watching the sun dip lower in the sky. I promised myself that next week I would get on the train to go see Mom, but I made that promise every week, and by now I knew I was full of shit.

*   *   *

When I got home, a thin layer of smoke and the overwhelming scent of tuna drifted through the house. Pixie stood in front of the open oven, pulling out the source of both. Dad was at the kitchen table, fanning the air with his newspaper.

I took in the scene from the doorway, some strange dream in which an alien had come to replace my mother.

"Pixie made tuna casserole," Dad said. There was a hint of an apology in his voice. "How was Mom today?"

"She's—you know. The same."

Dad smiled, but the corners of his mouth were downturned.

Pixie put the casserole on the counter. "Have a seat! We're just about ready for dinner."

I sat at the table and noticed the fourth chair was filled too. Father Skeeter was perched on the seat back, picking at a talon with his beak.

Pixie passed us each a plate. The mess of tuna and butter noodles was a murky shade of gray, burnt around the edges. Dad and I had mostly been eating canned tuna on crackers for dinner since Mom had been in the hospital. I was tired of tuna generally, and this version was somehow even less appealing than scooping it straight from the can. When Pixie sat, I noticed she was wearing Mom's apron: white canvas with a bumble bee emblazoned on the breast pocket.

My body tensed up. I turned to my dad. "Why is she wearing that?"

Dad looked at Pixie, then at me. His mouth opened but nothing came out.

Pixie widened her eyes. "I found this in the closet and assumed it was for anyone."

"Well it isn't," I said. "Take it off."

"Charlie—" my dad started.

"Take it off. Now."

Pixie untied the apron and slid it over her head. She folded it into a tight square. My hands shook as I took it from her.

"I'd like to lead us in grace now, if you don't mind," Pixie said.

I pushed my chair back and stood up, throwing the apron onto my chair. The movement startled Father Skeeter, who began flying circles overhead.

"Bless us, O Lord," he said.

"I'm not fucking doing this," I said.

"Language," Dad said.

"No, don't fucking *language* me. I'm not sitting here playing house with this freak and her deranged bird."

"Charles, sit." Pixie spoke with the stern voice of a priest in the confession booth, like she was ready to tell me how many Hail Marys to do for absolution.

"I'm not hungry."

I left them at the table and went outside. I didn't have anywhere to go, so I walked back to Beer World and sat on the bench, exactly where I'd been twenty minutes before. I felt like if I didn't get out of there, I was going to do something terrible. I had flash images of wringing the bird's neck, smashing all the shit in Pixie's bag. I wanted to swing a baseball bat at something, beat something with my hands until it softened to dust.

I opened my phone and texted the only person who came to mind. *Wanna grab pizza tonight?* I typed, then sent it off to Joey-Jim.

We hadn't hung out outside of work before. I wasn't sure why he was the person I reached out to. Maybe I felt bad because of how I'd acted earlier. Maybe I just wanted to be around someone who barely knew me, who I didn't have to act any type of way around.

Ten minutes passed, then: *Sure. When?*

Now? I'm still at beer world

He texted back right away. *Ok. Be there in a few.*

*   *   *

Joey-Jim's car was small, with cloth seats and an aux cord hanging out of the tape deck, instantly dating it as something nearly as old as us. He danced his fingers nervously across the steering wheel.

"Thanks for picking me up," I said. Now that I was actually in his car, I wasn't sure why I'd decided to do this. Joey-Jim looked so kind. I felt like a stray shard of glass on a tile floor, waiting to wedge itself unexpectedly into the soft meat of someone's heel.

"Why were you still at work?" he asked.

I shrugged. "Nowhere else to go."

"You usually go to Philly on Mondays, right? I feel like I heard you say that before."

I didn't remember telling him that. For whatever reason, I seemed to tell this lie a lot, as if saying it to everyone would make it true. "Oh, yeah. I didn't go today."

"What's in Philly?"

I stared out the front windshield at the stretch ahead: a Burger King with a sign announcing that *chicken fri s are b ck!*, a not-yet-finished bank, two rival gas stations that had beaten out a third. I did everything but look at Joey-Jim. "My mom," I said finally.

Joey-Jim nodded like he understood. "Ah, divorced parents. Me too."

"Actually no. Mine are still together."

"So, what's your mom doing in Philly then?"

I let out an uncomfortable laugh. "I was sort of hoping you wouldn't ask."

"We don't have to talk about it if you don't want."

"No, it's okay. She's at Penn. The hospital. She had a bad accident and has been there since. Actually, we both did. I'm all right but she's… Anyway, I try to go see her, but I don't get out there as much as I should."

"Shit."

We were both quiet for a minute.

"The pizza spot is up here on the left," I said.

"I'm really sorry."

"Don't be sorry. Just don't miss the turn. I'm hungry."

We pulled into the pizza joint. Joey-Jim ordered and when the pizza guy asked for a name, I felt surprised to hear him say Joey. I laughed.

"What?" he asked.

"Nothing. I'm just realizing if we're hanging outside of work, I can probably just call you Joey."

"Jesus, yes, please do. Joey-Jim is such a stupid fucking name. And you know Jim isn't even my middle name?"

We were both laughing, and I felt a loosening up inside me, a fist unclenching.

The pizza guy brought the box to the car, and Joey pulled it through the window, placing it on my lap before driving away. We drove around aimlessly, eating pizza and talking about whatever. I watched him laugh with grease dripping down his chin and felt more at ease than I had in a while. We finished half the pizza by the time we pulled back up outside of Beer World.

"You know, I was kind of surprised you asked me to hang out. You've been kind of a dick since…" he trailed off, let me fill in the gap.

"Have I?"

"Oh, come on."

I chewed my lip. "I'm not sure I'm up for anything more than hooking up, is all. I didn't want to give you the wrong idea."

"Don't do that. I never asked you for shit. Maybe I just want to hook up too."

"Do you?"

"I don't know. I'm still figuring that out."

"Why'd you agree to come then? If you think I'm a dick?"

"I never said I thought you were a dick. Just that you were acting like one."

I smiled in spite of myself.

"Well, I'm glad you did, anyway. Ask me to hang." He put his hands in the air. "Don't take it wrong. I'm not saying I think we're dating now or anything."

"All right, come on." I swatted his hands down. "You don't have to do all that."

I opened the car door to get out, but then a thought came over me that I couldn't shake. "Hey," I said, "would you wanna do something really fucking stupid with me on Friday?"

He raised an eyebrow. "What exactly did you have in mind?"

"I don't know how to put this, but have you ever heard about the parakeet minister around here?"

"What the hell are you talking about?"

"All right," I said, closing the car door. "You're not gonna believe this shit."

*   *   *

The week passed too slow. I avoided Pixie and Father Skeeter as best I could, though they didn't make it easy. Pixie was cooking all the time, nearly burning the house down. For someone with such poor kitchen skills, she couldn't seem to keep herself away from it. Every night from the foot of dad's bed, I could hear them practicing sermons in my room. Or at least, I could hear Pixie prompting the bird. He was too quiet for me to hear his replies.

When Friday rolled around, I texted Joey to make sure we were still on. I'd explained everything to him—the renting, Pixie, Father Skeeter. We'd researched the when and where of Father Skeeter's sermons. It wasn't too hard to find the church—if you could call it that, given that it was just some guy's basement. Turned out there weren't a lot of bird ministers or priests name Skeeter. He had a Facebook page with forty-two likes that posted religious quotes, "candid" photos of Father Skeeter at the pulpit, and graphics featuring the time and location of his sermons, which were shockingly frequent—three times a week, Friday to Sunday. The most recent post said his next sermon would be on forgiveness, held on Friday at 6pm. Joey agreed to drive me there. I told him I just wanted to see what it was about, but it was more than that. Something had been bubbling up in me since I saw her in my mom's apron, and maybe even before. Since she first mentioned my mom's name, or arrived at my door, or before I even met her.

Maybe I'd been simmering for months. I wanted to intrude on her like she'd intruded on me. To show up and disrupt *her* life. See how she liked it. I was still having violent thoughts, images of squeezing Father Skeeter till he popped in front of the congregation like a balloon full of guts. I didn't *want* to do that. It was just something that passed through my mind, a building pressure I struggled to release.

Joey picked me up at five thirty. "Ready for church?" he said.

"As I'll ever be."

The house was a short drive away. It was an unassuming place: a rancher, gray with a blue door. We parked across the street. As we walked to the door, I grew simultaneously more uncertain about this decision and more stuck inside of it. I was glad Joey was with me. I thought having him there made me less likely to do anything that would land me in jail. Though I couldn't be entirely sure.

The man who opened the door was tall and lank with thin-rimmed glasses and long, gray hair tied back in a ponytail. He looked like exactly the kind of guy who would host a bird church.

"You here for the service?" he asked. "I don't think I've seen you before."

"Yes," I said. "Pixie is my, um. Roommate?"

"Oh, shit! You're Charles?"

How this man already knew my name was beyond me. "It's Charlie, actually."

"Nice to meet you, Charlie. I'm Rand. Pixie's doing a special service for your mom today. She'll be so glad you're here."

He ushered us inside, down a hallway with peeling wallpaper and water stains dotting the ceiling. Rand led us down the stairs into a basement with mismatched benches set up like pews. Father Skeeter was preening in his cage, displayed on a small table beside a music stand at the front of the room. A clip-on microphone was attached to his cage wiring, the transmitter resting on the table. Fifteen or so people milled about. I didn't see Pixie among them.

Rand placed a hand on each of our backs. "Have a seat." He walked to the front and addressed the small crowd. "Thanks for coming, everyone. Please take your seats so we can get started. We have a really special sermon for you today."

People shuffled about, moving toward the benches. Joey pointed to the bird cage. "Is that Father Skeeter?"

"The very same," I said.

Rand placed a hand on the bird cage. "Father, could you get us started, please?"

The bird rocked back and forth, making strange, long chirps. Everyone leaned forward in their seats, craning to hear. Rand knelt in front of the cage and adjusted the microphone, which crackled to life and sent the chirps projecting through the room. Joey grimaced at the sound.

From behind me, I heard footsteps and turned to see Pixie walking down the aisle. When she got to the front of the room, she caught my eye in the crowd. If she was surprised to see me there, she didn't let on. She nodded, almost as if she'd expected me, and stepped up to the mic.

"Today," she said, "Father Skeeter is going to speak about guilt. But first I want to tell you a story about a woman I know. She's not well. A car accident left her in a coma."

The congregation let out a sympathetic *hmm*. I could feel Joey looking at me, but I didn't look back.

"I recently moved in with her husband and son. As many of you know, Father Skeeter and I consider ourselves nomads. But something called me to this home. When I saw their room for rent, Father Skeeter began chirping nonstop. I knew that God had spoken to him, and that we were meant to go."

I felt myself growing hot, furious. My jaw clenched. I was worried that if she kept going, I would do something I'd regret.

"I prayed over her photograph. That night, she appeared to me in a dream in which we met in her hospital room. She said she'd heard my prayers and thanked me. She said no one had prayed for her in some time, and asked me why I had. The reason, I said, was because I felt she needed it. At this she started to cry."

I became lightheaded, my stomach sick.

Joey leaned over to me. "Are you okay?"

I nodded, unable to get out any words.

"She told me her son hadn't come to see her in some time. She wasn't mad, but concerned. She knew it was hard on him and wanted to know how he was doing. I answered her honestly. I told her he was angry. Not at her, but at the world, and at himself. That he is punishing himself over something he can't change."

I stood up. Joey touched my arm, but I brushed him off.

"Charlie," Pixie said. The congregation turned to me. Out of tune with what was going on, Father Skeeter started chirping his hymnal again.

I stepped forward, struggling to breathe.

"She isn't mad at you. Your guilt is a trap."

"Guilt is a trap," Father Skeeter echoed. He did a little flutter and began to sing "guilt" with enthusiasm. A few people in the congregation started clapping along uncertainly, unsure if this was part of the show.

I stepped toward the stage in a way that must have appeared menacing, because an emaciated man in the front row threw his arm out and said, "Step away from the priest." But when he saw the look on my face, one that must have told him I would plow down anyone in my way, he dropped his arm and muttered an apology.

"She doesn't want you to blame yourself, Charlie," Pixie said.

"Blame, blame!" Father Skeeter chirped.

"Shut up!" I said.

A few congregation members gasped. I leaned over to look Father Skeeter in the eyes. I was feverish, my pulse throbbing in my chest, my neck, the tips of my fingers.

"Blame!" Father Skeeter said. His head bobbled from side to side. "Guilt, guilt, guilt."

I narrowed my eyes at him. Who the fuck was he to tell me what I felt? He was a goddamn bird. A bird couldn't know what guilt was or wasn't.

Pixie reached out and grasped my wrist. "You should go see her."

It was too hot, too loud. Father Skeeter was so close to my face. His ammonia scent made my stomach churn.

"She doesn't want you to keep punishing yourself."

I heard Joey call my name. He walked up the aisle and placed his hand on my shoulder. "I think we should go," he said.

I stared at the bird, almost believing he might tell me something transcendent.

"Forgive," Father Skeeter said. "Forgive."

Vomit shot up my throat and out, too suddenly to stop it. It splattered across Father Skeeter, who started flapping wildly around his cage, squawking. The congregation gasped. Someone shouted to get water and a towel for Father Skeeter. My brain flickered. I felt Joey lift me up by the armpits as everything went black.

*　　*　　*

I came to in Joey's car, stretched across the backseat. It was dark out. The congregation was filing out of the house and into their cars, though I didn't spot Pixie.

"You're up." Joey turned around from the front seat. "That was… intense."

"I shouldn't have done that. I don't know what came over me."

"I don't know. I think the bird had a point." The smile on his face told me he was both joking and not.

"Forgive, forgive," I said. We both laughed. But in my head, I saw myself standing at the edge of the burning car, not moving. Sitting outside Beer World instead of at the hospital. Throwing out my college acceptances, offering up my room, walling out Joey. I felt insane for thinking it, but it had seemed, for a moment, like the bird was seeing something inside of me and asking me to pull it out.

I pushed myself upright. "Hey, are you working tomorrow?"

"No. Why?"

"I know you probably don't want to go on any more errands with me after this one," I started.

He laughed. The sound was starting to feel familiar, a comfort.

"Would you drive me to the hospital when I get off work? To Penn? I haven't… it's been a while since I've gotten out there to see my mom. And I—" I felt a knot tangling in my throat. I tried to cough it out.

"Of course," he said. I met his eyes and could see he didn't need me to explain. We sat for a moment in silence, nothing but the hum of the car engine. I thought of Father Skeeter. *Forgive, forgive.* I wasn't sure who I was forgiving or for what. Everything had gone off the rails, and I'd been so busy being angry at the world that I kept spinning the tires deeper into the mud. I was glad I puked on the bird. It might have been the first real thing I'd done in a long time.

When we drove away, I stared out the window and watched the roof of the bird church pass swiftly by, then disappear.

*   *   *

I went straight to the shower when I got home, dodging Dad's questions about why I took my shirt off the second I walked through the door. Once I was clean again, I found Dad watching *Wheel of Fortune* in the living room, two bowls of stovetop mac and cheese on the coffee table in front of him.

He looked up at me. "What was that all about?"

"Puke. I'll explain later."

He nodded toward the mac and cheese. "Need some food?"

"Sure, thanks." I could feel him staring at me as I sat. "Why are you looking at me like that?"

"I want to talk to you about something." He pressed his lips together and took a deep breath. "I know you haven't been going to see Mom when you say you are." He said it very matter-of-fact, like he wasn't angry but had decided it was time to clear the air. Still, I felt like he'd stuck a pin in my lung.

"How did you know?"

"Because I was worried about you, so I asked one of the nurses if you seemed okay when you were there. And she said they hadn't seen you in over a month."

My apology came out in a whisper, a knot forming in my throat.

"You don't need to apologize. I just want to know what's going on with you. You haven't been yourself."

My eyes felt hot. I rested my face in my hands, trying to obscure that I was crying, but of course he knew. He put an arm around my shoulder.

"I keep wanting to help, but instead I'm just making everything worse," I said. "And nothing I'm doing is helping Mom get better."

He ran his hand over my hair. "Charlie, you can't think like that. There's nothing you could've done. I'm sorry I—I haven't been paying enough attention."

I sat up, wiping my eyes on my arm. "I'm going to see her this week. A friend is driving me into the city."

"Okay." He rubbed my head again. "Only if you feel up for it."

"I do. And maybe next time you go, if you want, I could go with you."

"Okay. I'd love that."

"And there's something else. I think I messed up with Pixie. Like, she might be really mad."

He gave me a concerned look, the kind of face that's asking a question.

"I might've maybe gone to her church and caused a bit of a scene. And puked on Father Skeeter. But that part was an accident!"

Dad rubbed his face, shook his head. "All right. That's all right. You should just apologize. I'm sure it'll be fine."

"Is she home?"

"I didn't see her come in, but you can go check."

I headed down the hall. The door to my old bedroom was closed, but light crept out around the frame. I knocked and waited. When she didn't answer, I pushed the door open slowly. Inside, the room was completely empty. The light was on, but there was no Pixie, and none of her stuff either. Her bag and the bird cage were gone. The bed was made, the dresser drawers half-opened and cleared out. I stood there for a moment, then called for my dad.

He came quickly, concerned by the sound of my voice, then stopped when he saw the empty room. "What the hell?" He stepped inside, pulling the drawers all the way open, as if her things might reappear if he only looked harder. "When did she even… I was here all night!"

"Did you fall asleep or something? Maybe she snuck in and out?"

He stood in the middle of the room, his hands on his hips, shaking his head. "I mean, maybe, yeah. I must've."

"I'm sorry. This is probably my fault."

Dad looked at me, pulling himself out of his confusion. He waved his hand in the air. "That lady was batshit anyway."

On the bed, I noticed something sticking out from between the pillows. It looked like a sliver of paper, maybe a note. I pointed to it. "Looks like she left something."

Dad reached out and grabbed it, holding it up. It was a piss-yellow feather.

"Nope," he said. "Just a little parting gift from Father Skeeter."

I plucked it from his hand and rolled it between my fingers, the colors rippling in the shifting light. I saw myself in front of the bird cage, Pixie's hand on my arm. It felt as if it had been a dream. Tomorrow, I would see my mother, and it would hurt. I would tell her about the minister bird and hope that somewhere in there, she could hear me, and it would make her laugh. Or maybe tonight, after everyone was asleep, she'd visit Pixie, and by the time I told her the story, she'd already know. I didn't believe in any of that shit, yet I couldn't shake the feeling that something had happened to me I couldn't explain. That years from now, I'd tell the story of the woman who appeared and dissipated like magic, and wonder if she'd even existed at all.

I placed the feather on my bedside table, deciding I would keep it. Proof, for my future self, I hadn't dreamt it up.

KATIE HENKEN ROBINSON *is a Boston-based writer and the Senior Editor at Electric Literature. Her writing has appeared in or is forthcoming from* The Southwest Review, Split Lip Magazine, *and* Grist, *among others. The winner of the 2025 Tennessee Williams Festival Fiction Contest and a Virginia Center for the Creative Arts Fellow, Henken Robinson's* *short stories have been finalists for numerous prizes and awards, including The Perkoff Prize and The Stephen Dixon Fiction Prize. You can find her at katiehenkenrobinson.com.*

Rolling Calf

Stephenjohn Holgate

My grandmother would tell me stories on the nights that my mother worked late, or was studying, or was with Butchie. She would chop jackass rope finely, stuff her pipe, even though my mother hated the smell of tobacco, and tell me a wild tale of Bredda Anansi or Bredda Tacuma or King Tiger. My favorite stories were the duppy stories that she wasn't supposed to tell me. I would beg her as she prepared her pipe, and she would laugh and say, "You love frighten youself, don't?" and I would smile and curl up next to her ready to be told about Old Higue and Whooping Boy and Three Foot Horse and River Mumma.

But the one that frightened me most was the Rolling Calf. I would close my eyes and see the red glowing eyes, the flames from its nostrils. I could feel the hot, sulfurous breath across the back of my neck, on my cheek. And the sound of the chains being dragged across the floor as the Rolling Calf came for me. Of course, I'd wake screaming and the next time my mother had to leave me with my grandmother she would say, "Stop fill the boy head with duppy story. Him growing up too fraidy-fraidy."

And my grandmother would laugh and smile and wait until my mother was gone before saying to me, "You know how to make sure Rolling Calf don't catch you? You know them like molasses and you can drop money for them to count? And that salt will keep them away? And if you have a knife you must stick it in the ground because then them won't able to follow you."

I would feel better then and help my grandmother shell pigeon peas or peel bananas for dinner while she told me about why the johncrow has a bald head and why Anansi's bottom is so big.

"You must know the story them, pickney," she would say to me. "The story them guide and protect."

I liked it when my mother went to work or to her classes, because she would return early enough to see me before I fell asleep. She would sing me a song or just come and give me a kiss on my head. But when she went out with Butchie, she always came back when I was already in bed, eyes long closed. Once, I woke up and heard my mother and grandmother speaking.

"That man science you?"

"No Mummy. Of course not. Why you say that?"

"Because from you start see him you forget you have one pickney. Forget that you have plans. So it must be obeah."

"I don't forget nothing. Nothing don't change."

"What him promise you? House and land and car and pretty frock? Like him promise every woman that come before you? And what them woman doing now? You know any of them with house? Land? Anything? You think you know Butchie, but you don't know nothing."

"What about Linval? Him sleeping?"

"Leave the boy alone. Make him rest. But make me tell you something. Nothing good going come of you and Butchie, you understand?"

Butchie was a big man with voice that was deep and loud. I would hear him holding court in his bar every afternoon as I walked from school. Usually about his plans to develop the area. Everyone knew Butchie was always buying up chunks of land here and there. Sometimes by offering a good price, sometimes by other means. I would hurry past the bar, often failing to look as I crossed the busy intersection by the ice cream shop. My grandmother always warned me about this, saying, "Those minibus driver down that road like the devil on them tail. Mind how you cross the street there."

But no minibus driver frightened me as much as Butchie's laugh did. Butchie's laugh made the countertop in his bar rattle. It was the kind of laughter that announced itself to everyone. And at the same time it had an otherness to it, like the creaking of bamboo at nighttime, or the howling of wind during a hurricane. It was a laugh that suggested a problem to be faced once silence fell. A portentous and thick laugh. Because everyone had heard the story about what happened when Butchie stopped laughing.

Everyone knew that Butchie, whose real name was Edward, had always kept rottweilers. Hulking beasts allowed to roam well beyond the boundaries of his land. One night, Butchie's dogs killed three goats belonging to his neighbor. When the neighbor complained to Butchie, Butchie had laughed and said, "Your fault for not looking after you goat them." The neighbor went home and poisoned the goat meat. The next night the dogs returned to the neighbor's property, ate the flesh of the goats they had killed, fell ill, and died. Butchie arrived shortly after losing his dogs and banged on the neighbor's door. The neighbor told Butchie he should have been looking after his rottweilers.

Butchie wasn't laughing when he struck the neighbor in the face or when he went to his car and brought back a sharp ratchet knife. He didn't laugh as he butchered the man's remaining goats, hanging them in a tree at the front of the property. The screams of the goats, who had to watch as each of them was killed, rang through the neighborhood. Blood pooled on the ground, a thick metallic stench filled the air.

"Next time you provoke me," Butchie said, "I going string you up just like I string up you goat them."

The man eventually sold his land to Butchie and moved away. Everybody stopped saying Edward and started calling him the Butcher or Butchie. He loved the name, loved the fear it inspired.

This was the story I was thinking about when I saw Butchie pick my mother up for their first date. I thought of screaming goats and pools of blood. I looked at Butchie, smoking a cigarette, its red tip glowing in the early evening's dark and thought of the glowing eyes of a Rolling Calf, the glint of Butchie's necklace like the chains it was said you could hearing clanking along the ground when the Rolling Calf came for you. I burst into tears.

"Donna, you pickney don't want you to go out tonight," Butchie said, laughing.

"Don't worry, Linval, you will see me later. Is not like I leaving forever," my mother said to me.

She didn't return until I was tucked into bed having terrible dreams. After that, things seemed to move quickly. From one night, to two nights, to three nights a week my mother was out. I saw her less and less, and during the little time we got to spend with each other, she was tired and irritable.

"That man replacing you one pickney," my grandmother said.

"Is not like that, Mummy," my mother said. "Him helping me."

"Helping you to form fool. I trust him about as much as I would trust a mongoose with one of me fowl them."

Still, my grandmother agreed to have Butchie come over one night for a meal. So that, in my mother's words, she could see the good that lived in him. It didn't go as well as my mother hoped.

Butchie came in smelling of rum and cigarettes, laughing and spreading himself across the little sofa that my grandmother had in her small front room. He continued drinking rum and speaking loudly, barely stopping to listen to what anyone else was saying. Somewhere between my mother clearing the plates from the main meal of boiled banana and steamed snapper, and her bringing in the sweet potato pudding, my grandmother turned to Butchie and said, "Butchie, I don't care what me daughter say, me spirit nuh take you. I can't stop her from seeing you. But you not coming back to my house after tonight."

Butchie, his face dark in the evening's shadows, standing on the veranda and smoking a cigarette, looked in at my grandmother, sat at her table, small, but fierce, and said, "You come in like Old Higue. Just old and dry up and miserable. No wonder you husband drop down dead. You suck out him life with you tongue, with the complaining. Better him dead than live with a miserable old witch like you. But you can't live forever. See if I don't walk through this house the day after them bury you."

And he pulled hard on the glowing cigarette, before throwing it to the ground crushing it under his foot.

"Babes," he called to my mother. "Me come check you tomorrow. Me have little business to deal with."

Before my mother could return from the kitchen we heard his car rattling to life and screaming off into the night.

"What you say to him?" my mother asked, wringing a tea towel in her hands. "What you say to upset him?"

Hot tears ran down my mother's face as she turned and went back into the kitchen.

But Butchie came back the next night, though my grandmother wouldn't allow him into the house, and the next night, and the next. Before long we found ourselves living at Butchie's place, halfway up the big hill I used to pass on my way to school. Butchie's bar sat at the bottom of this hill and each afternoon I would pass it with my head down, trying not to look in at the toothless old men drinking rum and playing the poker box. Once I heard someone call out, "Butchie, no you new boy pickney that."

"No son of mine could so soft. But is all right I going toughen him up," I heard Butchie say and then that rasping, deep, awful laugh filled my ears as I hurried up the hill.

Every day I had to get back straight after school because Butchie expected a long list of things to be done before he came home for dinner. I had to sweep the yard and wash the car. The fridge needed to have two full bottles of ice water. If they were half full, I had to fill them up early so they would cool down before Butchie returned, and if meat needed defrosting I had to defrost it. I had to feed the dogs, tidy the house, make sure the floor was swept.

Once, early on in the new regime of living with Butchie, my friends asked me to play marbles at the end of the school day. And I did. Then I went with them to pick guavas from Mr. McFarlane's trees, the ones that were in the opposite direction to Butchie's house. Then we went to skim stones down by the river. I forgot what time was, what the things I needed to do were.

When I reached home, Butchie was waiting. Seeing me, he pulled deeply on his cigarette, walked up to me and grabbed my arm.

"Boy. Where you been?" he asked. And not waiting for a response he said, "If you don't do the things that you supposed to do before I reach this yard I going bust you rass. You understand?"

Butchie's words were hot and felt as if they might burn me up on the spot. He sucked on the cigarette again and took it from between his lips. He held the burning tip just above my skin where I could feel its white heat.

"I promise you mother not to do anything this time. You lucky she inside the house," he said. "But next time I taking a whole pack of these and putting them out on you, one by one, until you learn some manners."

He threw me to the ground and walked back into the house shouting, "You spoil that boy, Donna. Him growing up soft."

I saw my mother look through the bedroom window. Her heavy, tired face. And then her eyes shifted from me and she was gone.

I was never late to do my after-school chores again.

I became convinced that Butchie was a malignant, supernatural force. A duppy. A demon. A Rolling Calf. And I was certain that only through some extreme action could I save myself and my mother from this man. So the next time my mother made stew peas with pig tail, Butchie's favorite, I emptied half a jar of salt into his bowl and stirred it furiously. I remembered my grandmother's stories, how a duppy could not abide salt, how it would cast them back to wherever they had come from. I watched as Butchie took a big spoonful of food. I watched his spluttering and coughing hoping that, finally, we would be free of him.

"You trying to poison me, Donna?" Butchie said pouring water into his mouth.

"Nothing wrong with my food, Butchie. Taste it," my mother said.

Butchie didn't taste her offered spoon, instead he turned his gaze towards me and, baring his teeth and flaring his nostrils, he said, "Boy, you think you funny? You think you can run joke with me?" And reaching into his pocket he pulled out his ratchet knife and flicked it open. Screaming, my mother grabbed Butchie's wrist and the knife flew to the floor. I jumped up from the table, picked the knife up and fled through the open door, not looking behind me, running all the way to my grandmother's house.

Later that evening, my mother turned up, arguing for my return, but my grandmother refused. I hid behind the door to our old bedroom and listened to them talking.

"You not taking Linval back to that place. I can't stop you from doing what you want because you is a big person. But if I let you take the boy that man going kill him."

"You exaggerating Mummy. Butchie was upset, but him wouldn't really hurt Linval."

"That you think. You think is only goat that man butcher? You can go take risk with your life, but you not taking me one grandpickney. You forget that him bury two wife already?"

My mother's face clouded and I could see that she was only just holding back thick tears.

"How you can keep my own child from me?"

"Because me partly raise him. Because you thinking only about youself and not about what is best for him. Because you promise to go sort out visa and look into getting work in foreign but everything fly out of you head since you pick up with that man. Because I will not allow that man to kill my one and only grandpickney."

They continued arguing in the doorway, my grandmother's small but powerful body blocking my mother from entering the house. I looked past them both into the dark outside and saw the glow of Butchie's cigarette, bright and threatening at the side of the road. I had escaped, but my mother was still trapped with this wicked man. Or this duppy wrapped in a man's skin.

Eventually my mother left, hunched and defeated. We heard Butchie's car splutter and cough its way up the road and once the sound died out my grandmother turned to me and said, "You want a chocolate tea?"

So for some time I stayed with my grandmother and my mother would stop by once or twice a week to plead for me to return. My grandmother had stopped blocking her; I had begun to refuse my mother's entreaties. I was feeling better and better about life, and I could see my mother getting thinner and greyer and more miserable, as if Butchie was sucking the life from her. Each time she came to the house she was a more diminished, frailer version of the person I knew.

One day, on my walk home from school, I passed Butchie's bar unthinkingly. Usually I ensured that I was on the other side of the road, only crossing back over after I had passed the intersection by the ice cream shop. But on this day, when the sun was hot and distracting, I daydreamed as I walked home, kicking rocks thoughtlessly and fingering Butchie's ratchet knife I had taken to carrying around with me. It was true that I was happier since living with my grandmother, but I still wanted my mother to join us. I missed her and wanted her to leave Butchie's possession and come back to living with us. The familiar booming, guttural laugh pulled me from my idle thoughts and when I looked inside, Butchie was there leaning against the countertop with a woman draping herself across his lap.

"When you going start look after me?" the woman asked.

"Cho. You know things complicated right now, baby."

"But you promise me."

"I need to deal with Donna and her mother first. Never think it would be so hard to get rid of that old witch. She just sitting in that house and not doing anything with it. But if she want me to force her out, is that going happen."

Then Butchie lifted his eyes, like two coals burning at the bottom of a fire, and realized I had heard everything he had said. I knew enough to run. I took off down the road kicking dust up behind me even as I heard Butchie growling and bellowing after me. My legs were young and swift and they took me quickly past the ice cream shop and into the intersection. I thought of the stories my grandmother had told me and pulled out the knife pushed into the cracked marl road.

I felt Butchie's thick, rough hand grab me before I could make it all the way up to standing. I thrashed and pulled and did my best to escape, but it was useless.

"Little foolish boy. You think you could escape me?" he said, squeezing his grip tighter. "At least you bring me back me knife. You want to see how it work? It sharp you know. I use it skin goat before. You want to see it skin something?"

A cold wash fell over my body. I knew Butchie would probably flay me there in the middle of the road, because Butchie feared no one. Because he was a Rolling Calf and no earthly laws could govern his behavior. Mustering what little bravery and strength I had, I swung my leg and kicked Butchie in his groin. He doubled over in the middle of the intersection and I ran to the other side of the road, turning only when I heard the horn and the screeching of tires.

My grandmother always warned me about the minibuses that tore through the town with no respect for other users of the roads.

"Them drivers fly about the place like leggo beast. Like say road code and law don't apply to them," she had said to me every time we crossed the road. "You must look for them, because them won't look for you."

And now one had finished Butchie's story. His great hulking body lay still in the middle of the road and a small group had gathered, gawping and bobbing their heads to see like johncrows around fresh carrion, to see if this terrible man were really dead. I saw the minibus driver hanging out of the window shouting obscenities at everyone, but I didn't stop to check on Butchie. I gathered myself together and ran home.

Later, in tears and carrying her clothes in cardboard boxes, my mother came home. My grandmother, asking no questions, folded her into her arms, and gave her space to mourn. I hid my joy, feigned sadness for her. I even allowed her to dress me up later and take me to Butchie's funeral. There, amidst weeping and wailing, I listened as speakers regaled Butchie as a pillar of the community who successfully ran a business and cultivated land. They described him as a developer, saying how he was well known and well regarded. I did not stand up and argue against these fictions, I just fingered the bag of salt in my pocket. Once at the graveside, where others would throw dirt, I would put salt. I knew how to make sure a duppy didn't come back to haunt anyone.

And after the digging of soft soil and songs of loss, when people were drifting off to grab plates of curry goat, and rice and peas, I bent down to empty my packet of salt around Butchie's grave. Looking up I saw my grandmother watching me. Her face broke into a broad smile as she reached into her handbag and pulled out her own container of salt. I helped her sprinkle it at every corner of the grave and we walked back to the house feeling easier in our steps.

__STEPHENJOHN HOLGATE__ was born in Jamaica and now lives in Aotearoa New Zealand. He holds an MA in creative writing from the International Institute of Modern Letters, Wellington. His work has appeared in West Trade Review, After Dinner Conversations, Decolonial Passage, Turbine, *and* takahē. *He is a 2023 PEN/Dau prize winner.*

He Said the House Was Haunted

Amelia Christmas Gramling

The first time he said the house was haunted, it was October. I laughed because it suited the season. But now it's March, and the weather has shifted toward superstition, winds high enough to level trees. And the joke, like the house, is no longer sturdy; I catch it bending towards belief.

The house is not old, but it was built to house the aging—what they call a "mother-in-law suite." An odd little half-house at the top of a hill on the edge of a horse farm. Haunted by a woman, or so we joke, who lived beyond the lifespan of her reason, who moved here when age reduced her to the sum of her needs.

Or that's the story we like to tell, because when we moved here, we were also enfeebled—not much more than need ourselves. And if the house is haunted, it's only because the history we thought we were uncovering behind the siding was not a stranger's but our own.

This house returns us to the one we came here to forget.

* * *

I loved him, first, in an attic apartment in Eastern Iowa: wood paneled, pitched ceiling, carpeted even in the bathroom. The apartment was an afterthought, a strange addendum to an old house, but it alone rose above the tree line. In the mornings, it was awash in light.

I think he would agree that in that period we felt like we were living outside the bounds of polite society. When we walked hand in hand through the college town, built within flooding distance of the Iowa River, streets wide enough for horse-drawn carriages and little else, we felt spotlit. If ever he kissed me in public, he'd murmur,

"We should be killed."

And then he'd kiss me while I laughed.

We moved fast. In retrospect, it was as if we knew what was coming.

*   *   *

We met in late summer of 2021 and were living together by Halloween.

In the early days, I couldn't distinguish my love for him from love of his attic. The tapered walls were covered with movie posters, signed photographs, and prints, like a sheet of one-way windows or a panel of trick mirrors. Every framed picture he'd hung up, a truer portrait of himself: movie monsters and monster movies; Boris Karloff and Bela Lugosi; Dario Argento and George Romero. The course he taught that fall and reprised in the spring was yet another autobiography, *Making Night Hideous: Drama as Haunting*. In it he taught *Hamlet* and Ibsen's *Ghosts*; Angela Carter's "The Bloody Chamber" and Shirley Jackson's *The Haunting of Hill House*. He lent me the latter early on, furred with sticky notes. I noticed that where the cover had once proclaimed *Now a Netflix Original Series,* S had Sharpied a still, black moon. S was like that: when the times didn't live up to his tastes, he scrubbed them from view.

If I asked him questions about himself, he was often evasive— he'd change the subject, make a joke. On more than one occasion, I asked him what he was thinking, and he answered, contemplatively,

"Poo." But if I turned his head, instead, toward his collection, he'd begin—slowly—to reveal himself. So, naturally, we were talking Hamlet's ghost when I learned that for S, our love was an interruption to grief. S's father had died the year before we met.

We were out on the fire escape of the attic apartment, sharing a cigarette, and watching the street. It was late. A man I'd seen before, a local character who was famous in town for wearing a duct-tape toga and little else, appeared under a streetlight. The man gestured dimly to something out of view. I said, under my breath, "He beckons you go away with him." S laughed before he corrected: "It. *It* beckons you go away with it." I rolled my eyes, but S was already full tilt: "No, no, hear me out. At first, it's just a mute shape in the armor of Hamlet's father. Horatio's not sure what *it* is, and neither is Hamlet. In fact, later, Hamlet tries to back off, deny the resemblance:

> '… *The spirit that I have seen*
> *May be a devil, and the devil hath power*
> *T' assume a pleasing shape; yea, and perhaps,*
> *Out of my weakness and my melancholy,*
> *As he is very potent with such spirits,*
> *Abuses me to damn me.'"*

(He really did quote these lines from memory. I know.)

"But when it walks, it beckons to Hamlet, talks to Hamlet alone—says *remember* and *revenge*.

"What's fucked up about the gesture," and here S stopped to beckon, "isn't just that it's Hamlet's father returned from the grave, but that it indebts him to *a past he wasn't there to witness*—a past about which he can never be sure, one that he can't confront, as you could confront a living father. The ghost, you know, is covered in armor. Hamlet can't even see its face."

S's estranged father had died suddenly, in the summer of 2020, during the height of quarantine. S had been living in the attic apartment when he heard the news. S watched the funeral over Zoom.

*   *   *

After he told me, we made love. I woke early to snoop. But in the blue/yellow half-light of morning, I saw the flimsiness of the posters that covered his walls, the places where the tape was peeling, taking with it drags of drywall. Maybe it was decoration after all. He ornamented his home in the trappings and the suits of hauntings, as a way of warding off his ghost.

*   *   *

For my part, I was looking to escape. I, too, was a collector but had little of my collection with me. A box of my things in my sister's attic in Kentucky. A box of my things in my ex's basement in Ohio. A box of my things in *his* mother's attic. And so on. I met S with all his objects apparently gathered in one place and felt the special pull, in early love, to anchor myself in someone else's things. And in the beginning, I succeeded. I disappeared into the furnishings, and tchotchkes, the collection of California Raisins, the tub with the detachable showerhead in the carpeted bathroom whose ceiling tapered to such an alarming degree that to take a shower meant squatting on your knees.

The kitchen was so small, it couldn't endure a fridge, so the fridge stood—not sane—in the hallway. In the morning, he made omelets, and his concentration was so intense that simply by walking into his periphery, or by saying his name ever so gently, I could make him jump out of his skin.

*   *   *

It was Christmas break when he fell ill. The days broke late and drifted wearily for a few hours in the winter half-light of the attic until they settled, like dregs, on the other side of the world. He had a persistent headache that lasted half a week. By the new year, he couldn't get out of bed.

II.

Love, like sickness, lives in that hazy half-light between choice and fate. Seduction is a spell, but who can be said to have cast it? S did a perfect impression of "The Monster Mash." I did a passable Groucho Marx, and in both cases we were really impersonating our mothers, who were impersonating the color TV.

When it comes to health, choice is also illusory. I was with S when CNN informed us that Johnson & Johnson baby powder was, well into the nineties, tainted with lead. When we heard—both of us inadvertently poisoned by our mothers—we shrugged.

So, with love. We think we say yes to a lover, make a choice about who we are and what we want, and in fact, we say yes to a stranger—not only the child he used to be, but the unfathomable other that love will become; it is all in the asking, all in the warning.

"You won't like it," says Dudley the caretaker of Hill House—which I read hungrily that January while S convalesced. "You'll be sorry I ever opened that gate."

*   *   *

He got sick a year into the pandemic. It wasn't just that those left in the medical profession had, by 2021, less patience for the illegibly ill, it's that the specter of COVID *had* made us—the public—jumpy, spooked, strangers to our own bodies. S was sick with something both invisible and vague. He was weak, exhausted, easily confused. He complained of a racing heart, migraines, of roving and unpredictable pain.

S did his credibility no favors by fashioning himself after Bryan Ferry. The first doctor I took S to in February wasn't charmed by S's fuchsia-colored high-waisted pants. In fact, the doctor was the picture of skeptical rationality in a military-style haircut. S told his story, and left the clinic, thirty minutes after arriving, with a diagnosis of Generalized Anxiety.

I recognized the category of (non)illness into which S had been shuffled from a show we'd started watching religiously that winter, after S got sick: *The Dead Files.*

When we first met, S and I watched films. In the Halloween season of 2021, we sampled the greatest hits of his DVD collection, which fulfilled the promise made by the posters covering his walls. After he fell ill, time elasticized, and we longed for a void into which we could mindlessly dissolve—i.e. reality TV. *The Dead Files* came on the Travel Channel and its subjects—haunted Americans—were selected based on letters they wrote in to self-proclaimed "physical medium" Amy Allan and her partner, former NYPD detective, Steve DiSchiavi. Often the families featured on *The Dead Files* were witness to strange phenomena, but also chronically "ill" with insomnia, fibromyalgia, cystic fibrosis, anxiety, depression, loneliness, and displaced rage. They were poor, white, and lived in places like Youngstown, Ohio, and Gary, Indiana—the postindustrial wastelands of middle America, the suburbs God forgot.

We watched *The Dead Files* for the same reason one might be tempted to email www.helpmedeadfiles.com: Our lives were disrupted by something mysterious, and we sought a common enemy, a place to put our own displaced rage. For those featured on *The Dead Files,* the enemies were "shadow people," hordes of "restless dead" that sent tendrils into the open mouths of sleeping children. For us watching, the enemy was con artist Amy Allan, and guilty-by-association sidekick Steve DiSchiavi.

Though we hate-watched Allan passionately because she deceived fretful widows into believing their moody adolescent daughters were possessed by demons, her methods were also intoxicating—because sometimes they worked. The families that wrote into *The Dead Files* were indeed cursed, because of the perfectly ordinary conditions of life where they lived: poisoned water, polluted air. For these people, Allan offered the sheer power of her belief. It wasn't a cure, but for those who suffered, she offered catharsis, absolution, and freedom from personal responsibility. "There's something wrong with me" was reconfigured on *The Dead Files* as "There's something wrong with the house," and so Allan left the haunted with hope: the possibility—if not the means—of getting out.

*   *   *

Of course, I believed S was sick. And yet.

I was—as weeks hardened into months—more and more seduced by the doctor's suggestion that what was wrong with S's body originated in his head. The prospect, once raised at the clinic, followed me back up the attic steps. *Was there a history of mental illness in his family? Had S ever struggled with bouts of prolonged sadness? Hopelessness? Loss of appetite?*

S wasn't insulted by the implication. He was incensed.

When we left the clinic, before I could ask a timid, "So how are you feeling?" S snorted derisively. "I could have been bleeding from the fucking eyeballs, and that hick would've given me a referral to a shrink. Anxiety my ass."

But in listening to the "hick's" questions, I realized how little I knew myself. What was the state, now that he mentioned it, of S's mental health? By the time we were walking up the attic steps, the rage had gusted through S. He made it to the blue couch, weakly loosened his tie, and collapsed.

Neither S nor I came from households which acknowledged the legitimacy of what is, today, commonplace pathology. When I was a girl and my mother didn't get out of bed for days at a time, no one said "depression." My dad said she was in a "black mood," "possessed" by something unnameable. We maneuvered through her moods as one maneuvers through the weather. I learned to batten down the hatches and wait.

I shared this fundamental skepticism with the participants on the *Dead Files*. Mental illness was, for them, a much less likely culprit than one of Amy Allan's so-called "gobliny goblins." Don't get me wrong, the participants on *The Dead Files* racked up both diagnoses and prescription drugs—but they, in almost every case, had little faith in doctors to pinpoint the real source. In Allan's universe, the source wasn't physical or emotional, but something altogether other: a foreign intruder, an evil force (sometimes extraterrestrial) which migrated to the family from a bad somewhere else. Narratively speaking, Allan and DiSchiavi would have preferred to locate the badness inside the home, to uncover a nineteenth century newspaper clipping from a local library which revealed a brutal killing had occurred in the basement, the bones of the victims buried under the cornerstone, but those histories were hard to come by in flyover country. The archives are slim. And the houses aren't that old.

S and I, marooned in our love, had no shared history. We were alone in that river town with the exception of the other. We had graduated from our MFA program and stayed behind an extra year while our friends moved away, moved on, moved out. In the attic apartment, history and reality rarely intruded. When it came to S's mental health, there was no one with whom I could triangulate what was normal and what was aberrant, what was old and what was new, what was symptom and what was cause, how much of S's personality was his illness, and how much was something closer to loss.

S was debilitated—and yet, as far as the clinician could tell—in perfect health. So I wondered with Amy Allan: Was something wrong inside the house?

*   *   *

At the beginning of March, I found him sitting in the dark, holding a worn red notebook filled with the previous semester's lecture drafts. He was close to tears. I curled in his lap.

"What's wrong?"

"I can remember writing this down, but reading it back is so strange. It's like I can't access that part of myself anymore. I feel like I'm reading someone else's words."

I looked down at the notes and realized that I remembered the lecture he was referencing.

In the fall, before S got sick, I sat in on one of his *Hauntings* sections.

He began that class with a question: "What's the difference between grief and mourning?" And eventually the class arrived, through his coaxing, at the answer he liked: time.

Mourning was a period. It was dramatic, contained action, and might be structured as an arc. Grief wasn't so easily moved, concluded, or exorcised. He wrote a word on the board and circled it: "Contretemps." Counter-time.

"As Derrida reminds us, the ghost, at its first appearance, is already a repetition. It's visited the ramparts before Hamlet arrives and before *Hamlet* begins. Hamlet can't remember when his father died, can't locate the loss in time—there's no way to know or to measure mourning's start or end. It's always extending itself, backwards and forwards, muddling the dates, covering its tracks. *The time is out of joint.* Hamlet believes that by letting the ghost take possession, by giving himself over to the demands of the past at the expense of the future, he can go back and impose order on the disorder, serve as a corrective, *set it right*."

A pause, then quietly, S, from the present, said, "I'm just so afraid it will never come back."

I shushed him and lied.

III.

S got sick in January. By May, I had gone a bit mad.

After the first doctor had diagnosed S with anxiety, we sought a second opinion. Now, the going theory was that S was one of those poor souls who had developed Long COVID, which seemed, as far as I could tell, as nonspecific and ephemeral a diagnosis as nineteenth century hysteria. I joined a chatroom and drank in horror stories. Out of work for six months, twelve months, two years. Brain fog. Heart palpitations. Loss of sex drive. Divorce. Depression. And—in rare cases—suicide. I bought a rolling subscription to Zinc, Niacin, and Vitamin B12. I sent someone in Sacramento sixty bucks for a twelve pack of FODMAP smoothies that never arrived.

I became manic about taking walks.

*   *   *

Amy Allan, when it comes to recovery, has only two modes, one of two prescriptions for dealing with ghosts: Stay or go. Most of the haunted who ask for her help don't have the means to pick up and leave, but Allan, in almost every case, confesses it would be preferable, safest, most elegant, to abandon everything they know and flee. Bulldoze the house, salt the earth, start over somewhere else.

Indeed, it would have been simpler if S—once struck with illness—was always confined to the worn blue couch, but he had his good days. We got out. I managed to convince myself on these "good days" that he was on the mend, that he was well enough to be coaxed into considering the future, into making plans. His lease would be up at the end of June. It was May. We still hadn't discussed what would happen to us when we reached that irremediable deadline, where we would go, and when we left, whether "we" would leave together.

Once, he gave in to my near constant solicitations that he join me for fresh air and exercise, and we went out for a walk above the Maquoketa Caves, north of town. We stooped and squatted through a dank passageway of hollowed earth and then emerged in the dripping spring sunshine, thawed. He grinned at me, from the other side of a shallow passageway and suddenly looked so very much like himself, I shivered with hope. But, by the time I'd reached him, the wind had shifted. He fashioned a cane out of a fallen tree branch and hobbled back to the car. It (or he) could turn like that, that fast, and when it did, as it always did, I was so wracked with fury, I had to hang back, duck out of view, bite my fist.

The youngest child of five, I was not used to mothering, to nursing the sick, to taking better than even cursory care of anyone— including myself. In truth, my mother had given me no fewer than four plants since I left home at eighteen, and I had neglected all four to premature death. Before I met S, I think I believed in the you-can't-find-me-if-I-shut-my-eyes logic of the child, that if I didn't learn (much less memorize) the domestic book of spells, if I couldn't cook or keep house, hold a baby in my lap, I could escape being needed at the expense of myself.

But then illness made S into a child, in the way that someday time will make children of us all. He sometimes reminded me of my grandmother—though I kept this to myself—diagnosed with dementia five hundred miles southwest. He repeated himself. He lost his keys, lost the thread. He thought in circles and walked in loops. I vacuumed the carpeted bathroom. I emptied the trash. I made the soup. I asked him, "How are you feeling?" I laid a hand on his forehead. He didn't ask and I didn't offer, and yet by May we were both more and less than friends and lovers.

I was his caretaker, and he was my charge.

One night, something (who can say what?) possessed him to rent *Burnt Offerings.* I watched Bette Davis—made prematurely old by a life-sucking Victorian summer home—grow forgetful, lose her marbles, stop trusting her own mind. I bit my nail beds through her swift deterioration. By Davis's penultimate scene, I was bleeding. I stood up, left the room, pretended to pee. When I returned, the screen was frozen on Davis's contorted face.

I wouldn't sit down until S agreed to tell me the ending. He refused.

Suddenly, I found myself shouting.

"You're not my father, you can't *make* me watch it."

"Are you serious?

"JUST TELL. ME. WHAT. HAPPENS."

"Fine—you really want to know? Everybody dies. They all die. The house eats the whole fucking family alive."

Just as suddenly, we were no longer discussing the movie. Subtext became text. I said more than I meant: "I'm just so afraid. *Aren't you afraid?* What if *this*"—I gestured to him on the blue couch—"is just how it is now?"

He heard in my elision the threat I both did and didn't mean and so threatened, himself: "Do you want to leave? Is that what you want? Well, no one is keeping you here. Be my guest."

And so, I left.

*   *   *

Hauntings remind us of the instability of binaries, the mutability of flimsy categories that separate self and other, here from there, this time from that time. Amy Allan's methods were seductive—get the fuck out—but they were also naive. Our ghosts won't remain where we left them. Between S and I—in that fight—were others. My mother, for one, who had come close to dying of breast cancer when I was a kid. S's father, for another, who had stormed out in rages throughout S's life, and then had gone and never come back. We were threatened by forces and figures invisible to the other, that took over in the heat of the moment.

I think we all know this to be true, in love, but I met S at a strange time both for love and for grief, when it seemed that, in the aftermath of the pandemic, there was no limit to that which, as far as the fearful public was concerned, could and should be quarantined.

I called a friend after I walked out of S's apartment, and she said, in my defense, that I didn't have to go back, that no one would blame me if I "chose myself."

She said, "Well, you know, you didn't sign up for this." And she was right.

But what do we sign up for when we choose to make a home with the other? Or, better question—for whom is love a choice, and how, once in love, does one impose such conditions?

S's illness coincided with a cultural fixation on boundaries, on categorizing and policing modes of relation, but in practice, those linguistic and theoretical partitions collapse at first touch. If I left, he would move into a one-bedroom condo in Yonkers with his mother, a mother who was busy mothering her own 103-year-old mother on her own blue couch. Whose is the love that stays put, confined to one room of the house?

I wasn't just wanted, I was *needed*. And I was, at times, infuriated by the imbalance between us. Not only for the reasons you might expect—because I felt unappreciated, taken advantage of, or because my love for him was coming at the expense of my work (I found myself nearing the end of a one-year teaching contract with no savings and no job prospects, and nowhere I could imagine moving toward). I *was* angry for those predictable reasons and in the predictable ways, but beneath that anger was something else: the knowledge that I had chosen him as an escape route, a way out of my own blank apartment. I had not been careful, in other words, about what I wished for. What if he got better? And what if, in getting better, he stopped loving me—his love no longer reinforced by the urgency of his need? Or—and this was a fear whose reality I could only very rarely brush up against—what if he didn't get better at all?

The truth is, he wasn't the only one of us pretending that June wouldn't arrive, that time wasn't operating by its usual rules, that by talking and walking in loops, we had created a stay we could live inside. I thought of my boxes, abandoned in other houses where I had played at other lives, and wondered what of myself would remain with me when I left the attic apartment behind.

I came back that night, and we held each other even more tightly, and I got the ice for his ice water, and I kissed his forehead. I promised myself I would—tomorrow—take control, force the both of us to face the future, but I knew, even then, that I was telling a lie.

*   *   *

We stopped watching *The Dead Files* after season seven, episode five, subtitled "The Consumed." Amy and Steve were called in to help Laurie of Youngstown, Ohio—Laurie, who had stage four cancer and two months to live.

Allan begins each episode with a "Night Walk" of the haunted house in question—which has been scrubbed, in anticipation of her arrival, of all personal touches, any trace of a life that might call the authenticity of Amy's psychic powers into question. Walking the darkened hallways at the start of "The Consumed," Amy said, "The thing about this land is that the dead can't die here. They're trapped." Concluding, in an accent that wanders the continental United States and parts of Canada, "So, there's something very wrong with this land."

That wrongness, Amy claimed, affected the living—and was even the source of Laurie's cancer. It had also, per Amy, engendered personality changes in the rest of the family. Laurie's daughter suffered "anxiety attacks." Laurie's husband seemed "possessed" and was often afflicted by violent rages, punching walls, chasing the dog around the house. At one point, Steve DiSchiavi, in a moment of surprising lucidity, asked Laurie if her husband's rage might be related to his grief. "You don't tink it's frustration," Steve said in his old school New York accent, "about youse and your sickness?" Laurie agreed that her illness could make her husband "frustrated" but couldn't, she said, cause him to become someone other than the man she married.

For Laurie, the possibility of haunting helped her to externalize her family's demons: divorced her daughter's anxiety and her husband's rage from one origin—her impending death—in favor of a story that preceded their arrival, may even precede the construction of the house. Laurie didn't, in emailing helpmedeadfiles.com, believe that Amy Allan or Steve DiSchiavi could save *her* (could cure her cancer or otherwise alter the doctor's prognosis) but she hoped they could contain the illness, the wrongness, to her body alone. She wanted to die knowing her death wouldn't disfigure her family for life. In other words, Laurie's was the ghost she hoped Amy could exorcise. She was asking for a proleptic exorcism. In another age, she would ask to be buried with a stake of holly through her heart, pinning her to the coffin floor. What Laurie wanted, simply, was for her loved ones to return to a world unruptured by grief, made clean of her and of her loss.

When Amy Allan walked into the dining room during her "Night Walk," she proclaimed that she had discovered the source of the haunting: "A big, like, blob? That's moving like a pulse?" At first, it seemed she was describing a heart, but as is often the case, Amy's metaphor soon got away from her. The blob was the "manifestation of all the negativity in the house." It fed on the sick, on suffering, it was touching the ceiling, and soon, it would "mesh" with the walls: it would *become* the house.

"Oh my God," S said, next to me, "She's describing a tumor metastasizing."

IV.

S dreamed of his father on the morning he started bleeding internally.

He hardly ever spoke his dreams aloud, and even more rarely spoke of his dad, but he told me this one, his hand cold in mine, after he woke from a fainting spell in the same small clinic—in the same small room—where, in February, he'd been first diagnosed with anxiety.

Now it was June.

I'd driven him through the midwestern soup, along the road that follows the river, after he called out from the attic's carpeted bathroom: "So, I appear to be shitting blood," and I agreed that sounded bad.

Military Haircut was nowhere to be found. Instead, a nurse practitioner with soft wrinkles around her eyes grabbed S by the shoulders, mid-swoon, to keep him from hitting the floor. I don't remember what she said to convince us an ambulance was worth the price of admission, but I got the gist: He was losing blood—fast.

S, a lapsed Catholic who worshipped at the church of Halloween, was superstitious, and less spooked by the blood loss than he was by the dream—which was just his father talking, the words he couldn't make out. S said that the dream wasn't scary, it was weirdly comforting—familiar. But, after he woke up, it was the comfort which scared him the most.

I played the skeptic, told him not to be silly, and I let the throbbing blob inside me grow a little fatter on his fear.

Later, after he'd been admitted to the hospital, and was awaiting a blood transfusion, I wandered into the cafeteria, contemplated the wisdom of the SunChips vs. the honey-spiced Fritos, and called my mom. I was calm as I briefed her on the "facts" of his condition, as far as I understood them—which was hardly at all—but my voice cracked when I told her about the dream. She became *my* skeptic, recited her lines with feeling: "It was just a dream." Then she elaborated. She said that S's body knew something he didn't (knew the wrongness was reaching a fulcrum, building steam), and plotted while he slept. The dream of his late father was not really his father, but his unconscious rising to the surface of conscious thought, assuming a questionable shape, doing what was necessary to scare him awake.

I didn't say but thought—that sure sounds like a ghost to me.

*   *   *

At the end of "The Consumed," as at the end of every episode, Allan and DiSchiavi moved onto "The Reveal" of their findings to the family. Amy's revelations were always terrifying, and usually they involved a detailed description of an army of dead people hovering around a baby's crib. But the "Reveal" was usually calibrated to make the family come apart at the seams, so that Amy, in prescribing her cure, could build them back up again, restore sanity, inspire hope. When a family couldn't afford to leave, her "cures" included the hanging of crystals, the sprinkling of expensive, exotic salts, and the solicitation of a hunky male medium or a generic "Holy Man"—sometimes both. Amy presided over an oddly, and inconsistently, secular metaphysical universe; the particulars weren't important. What the most desperate wanted to know was that someone was coming, someone could be called, that while the *infestation* was real, it didn't mean the house was condemned.

As was clear from the opening credits of season seven, episode five, *The Dead Files*, in responding to Laurie's call, had crossed an uncrossable line. Laurie's suffering was beyond the pale of "normal" hauntings, and as DiSchiavi repeated numerous times throughout the episode, her story was utterly "hawtbreaking."

After "The Reveal," of the all-devouring ghostly tumor, DiSchiavi said aloud what we were all thinking:

"Amy, listen, I don't want to put pressure on you, but I really hope you can come up wit something for Laurie, so she can live out her final days in peace."

In Steve's words, you could hear something like an admission to the hokum, to the scam, an indication that he was a conscience-stricken accessory to Amy's unchecked villainy. You got the impression, finally, that this was a human being stepping out of a role he was paid to inhabit and genuinely asking for mercy.

Amy Allan blinked twice, shook her head.

She did not extend mercy and she did not relent.

She told Laurie and her husband that if they stayed in the house, they'd be "eaten alive."

"What I'm honestly hoping," she said, "is that the area will be *leveled*."

Laurie, the postscript revealed, died a few weeks later, before the episode aired.

*   *   *

The new blood made him cold all over. I cracked a Dracula joke, and S indulged me, his smile cracking through his lips. He had finally been admitted to the ER after an interminable stint in the waiting room where we watched *Beat Bobby Flay* in between trips to the bathroom. I helped him from the wheelchair to the toilet and then stood outside and waited for him to signal that he was done—then wheeled him back to Bobby Flay grinning ghoulishly, spooning Fresno chili hot sauce into Guy Fieri's open mouth.

Now, S was recovering from blood transfusion number two. He slept while the machines recorded him sleeping. I, unsleeping, glutted myself on basic cable, curled up in two metal chairs pushed together, my butt sagging through the ever-widening gap.

In the ER, between the hours of midnight and 4am, ghosts abounded—Betty White for instance. The *Golden Girls* marathon on CMT inspired in me many revelations, only one of which I'll record here. It occurred to me that there is always a *Golden Girls* marathon playing on basic cable at 2am, and who is watching basic cable at 2am but the elderly and the infirm?

Golden Girls has taken the priest's place in the preparation of man for his end.

The next day, S was taken for tests to confirm the doctor's theory that the bleeding was coming from his stomach lining due to prolonged "ibuprofen abuse."

Basically, the doctor believed S was ill from taking over-the-counter pain relievers for the chronic pain he suffered due to Long COVID—an illness that, as far as the ER doctor was concerned—wasn't otherwise relevant to S's current condition.

It's easy to anticipate the story in which his illness turned out to be something metaphysical, that belief in his own illness, and its attendant anxiety, made him sick. Indeed, that is the story I anticipated, when S was wheeled away for his CT scan.

His mom, in the south of Yonkers, couldn't make the trip because she was still caring for her mother, and I realized, as S rounded the corner on the stretcher, and I brushed the hair from his forehead, and pressed my lips to his palm, how it happens in the worst lighting—in front of the TV, in the blue-tinged dark—we were each other's family now.

Death is the daily business of the hospital. So mortal fear, however acute, has little get-up-and-go; it eventually dulls and becomes boredom amid the ward-wide chorus of so many tiny beeps. After the test, we waited and watched *Reba*. We waited and listened to an old man in bed thirteen beg a nurse to play Al Jolson over the loudspeaker. We waited and listened to "Puttin' On The Ritz." We waited so long that waiting stopped being boring and became something else. At some point, it seemed clear to both of us that we wouldn't hear anything until the next morning.

I hadn't showered in forty-eight hours. S was on transfusion number three, and yet somehow, between the two of us, I looked the worse for it. I decided I would leave and come back first thing. I would indulge in much needed *self-care.* I would return to the attic. I would shower on my knees, spend the night in a real bed, and recover some of my lost sleep. I would celebrate my freedom by devouring a meal I knew S would hate. I had, in fact, just ordered from that Ethiopian place when S's newest doctor walked in.

The doctor was young, and wearing a mask which covered her carefully composed attempt at neutrality. She had something to say that she did not want to say. She avoided meeting my gaze.

There was a mass in his small intestine.

Cancer?

The question, once voiced, remained, like static, in background of the room.

My phone buzzed. "We've confirmed your order from I HEART FUFU."

"Well—" she said. She couldn't yet say anything for certain. She didn't dare say more.

Wait for surgery, the nurse cut in. Wait and see.

*   *   *

When the doctor bid us goodnight, I took myself to the bathroom. I bit the inner skin of my forearm to choke off my sobs. I told myself to stop. I told myself to lie. I washed the blood back into my face. When I returned, *Reba* was still playing to a muted room.

"So," I said.

"So" he said.

"Spooky."

And he nodded. I crawled into bed at his side. We watched Reba's mouth move, and we listened to the space between us, monitored by machines, murmuring out of sync, and he whispered, very, very quietly, "I don't want to die."

I told him over and over, with supernatural, practiced calm, that he was fine. That he had nothing to worry about—that things "like that" don't just happen.

But, of course, they do.

*   *   *

What I felt the next day, in those hours before and during his surgery, wasn't guilt or regret, but like there is such a thing as absolute reality, the world beyond mediation or meaning, and I was living, if only for a moment, on its northernmost end.

It made me think of *The Dead Files,* and I wondered if Amy might have been motivated by something other than cruelty for cruelty's sake. Peace of mind may have been a kindness, but it was also a lie: Laurie was being *eaten alive,* and in the wake of her death, her family couldn't stay in that house—couldn't live beyond the life as they knew it before Laurie died.

A tumor isn't depression and it isn't generalized anxiety. The body is ravaged and ravager at once. Some force, far greater than human will, takes over, and what I felt in that hospital room, for the first time in my life, was the awareness of time as a bodily function, an animal mechanism, that *it*, more than *I* was alive.

I sat with his blood-spattered turquoise pants in a plastic bag on my lap, and I watched a video I took of him singing in the attic apartment while beating an egg.

Fifteen seconds into the video, he noticed me filming, and stopped short, shot me that *look*, one dark curl loosed on his forehead. The look said: *What are you doing? This isn't for your someday enjoyment. It's just for now or not at all.* As a teacher, he believed something similar about the classroom, that a class had no value beyond the ephemeral, the time spent in the room, and that once it was gone, it was gone, *c'est la vie.* And, still, while I waited, I went against his wishes; I played him on a loop, I watched his joy turn to suspicion as he became aware of someone watching, recording over his shoulder, intruding on our private moment, like a house with eyes.

*   *   *

"So, it's benign?"

The prognosis would be delivered, as it turned out, rather anticlimactically.

I had driven S to his follow-up appointment, a catheter still strapped to his now hairless thigh, about a week after he was discharged from the ICU. A morose looking clinic doctor who was filling in for Military Haircut (on vacation it turned out) mentioned that the tumor wasn't cancerous, offhandedly, stopping just short of adding, "Duh."

The surgeon had taken, along with the tumor, about a foot of S's small intestine. According to the clinic doctor, the mass had been growing for months, but on that morning in June, it grew so large that his intestine telescoped in on itself, and S started hemorrhaging.

I remember blinking at the doctor blearily, unable to fully absorb this news. I asked him about S's Long COVID, and how it was related to the growth.

"Oh, no, he never had that."

What S had was a lipoma, a fatty tumor that only happens to the very young and the very old. The likelihood of his developing this condition was less than one percent. No rhyme, no reason, just a fluke.

According to the doctor—all of S's problems, his weakness, brain fog, his personality changes, the last five months of our lives—were symptomatic of this little foreign object, about the size of quail egg, growing in S's gut. So, the wrongness was removed, not by a hunky medium, a holy man, but a scalpel with brutal precision, slicing at the root.

When I expressed some measure of incredulity, the doctor met my gaze and shrugged.

"The gut is the second brain. You'd be surprised by how much it rules us."

Two and a half weeks later, S's lease was up. We moved.

*   *   *

I only have one picture of our last day in the attic apartment. S is smoking a cigarette (his first in months) in the foreground. He is more than a little gaunt, as though the mass that was taken was much heavier than the sum of its parts. The Iowa apartment is suspended behind him, as if from above. His eyeline draws even with the attic window. Already, there are things—the green of the blinds—I don't recognize.

While S was still "under the knife," my mom called with an escape route. She had been in touch with her neighbor and found us a place to land "for the time being, just as long as makes sense." S and I would move to Kentucky—to my hometown—to rent a cheap little half-house on the edge of a horse farm at the top of a hill, a five-minute walk from where I grew up. The apartment, originally a mother-in-law suite, was, as my mother mentioned to me several times, already built for a body in need.

*   *   *

At first—believe me—we were only joking.

S blamed her, "the ghost," when he lost his comb. I did the same when I shattered a glass or couldn't locate the title of a book. But then, we started noticing. Despite its many windows, the house was somehow weirdly bereft of light. We moved the furniture around. And we moved it again. I had trouble sleeping and began waking at 3am to take one of S's leftover anti-anxiety pills. Shadows in the corner of my eye flickered and dispersed. One morning, I smelled something and went into the backyard to investigate: A rotting deer's haunch had materialized as if it fell out of the sky. It was perfectly wedged, between two conjoined oaks. Difficult to take that as a *good* sign.

We didn't discuss why, but we never hung anything on the walls. Posters remained rolled in the tube. In the blank spaces we didn't cover with S's ghouls, goblins, and monsters, I sometimes saw things that didn't belong in that room.

*   *   *

In *The Dead Files* Amy Allan removes everything during her night walks that might undermine the legitimacy of her psychic connection to the afterlife. What she can't remove, she obscures with a black funereal veil. She walks the halls in the wee hours of morning. The landscape outside is strange, unrecognizable. She could be anywhere, at any time. Consequently, it is easy, when you marathon the show, to get the families confused.

Sometimes I felt like Amy Allan fumbling through the house scrubbed of my own presence, glimpsing apparitions, because I wanted someone else's story to answer for the fear that wouldn't remain behind where I left it. The worst thing that could have happened, didn't. I kept reminding myself, *we got away with something.* There was no room in the mother-in-law suite, in any case—no attic or basement, no nook, no cranny, hardly any closet space—to hold anything but relief.

And yet, I caught myself eyeing S suspiciously, asking him, "How are you feeling?" I found myself laying a hand on his forehead.

*   *   *

I was haunted by what didn't happen, and trapped in a moment that preceded the one I was in. But because the worst thing *didn't* happen, the loop wasn't closed, and the ending wasn't fixed.

Once, I reminded S, I forget why, about the dream he had in the hospital—the one about his father, the one that had terrified us both. To my immense shock, he smiled at the memory, getting it, or so I thought, completely wrong.

"Yeah," he said, "I knew when I saw him, that everything was going to be all right." Not all remembrances, not all visitations, are repetitions. Amy Allan would have us believe that we can only deal with apparitions in one of two ways—stay or go. But we can't outrun our ghosts—which is not to say that we must be haunted by them. There is also the possibility, as S once said to me, that you can follow Ophelia's prognosis instead of Hamlet's curse, *and wear your rue with a difference.*

*   *   *

One night, in the mother-in-law suite, the wind blew so hard that the power went, and I felt, rather than saw, him wake. From the darkness which, on the hill, was darker than anywhere I'd ever lived, we heard what sounded just like—though it couldn't be, could it?—a woman screaming.

We listened, our bodies taut.

Then my phone buzzed, and the room exploded with light. It was my mother, from down the street.

"Can you hear the foxes laughing?"

I read it aloud and S and I giggled until we both start weeping. A hand—who can say whose?—reached out from the dark.

AMELIA CHRISTMAS GRAMLING *is a writer and teacher from southwestern Kentucky. She received her MFA in Nonfiction Writing from the University of Iowa where she was awarded the Provost Postgraduate Fellowship for her graduating thesis. She now lives in New York. Her work can be found at* Bloodletter Magazine, Autostraddle, Bellevue Literary Review, *and elsewhere. She's drawn to stories that defy discreet eras of history: missing archives, found objects, and migratory ghosts.*

Each Other

Cristina Chira

When I called, you said you were in a bar near your office with Julius. You were waiting for him to finish up, then you would either go to another bar and give me the address or you would come home. When I asked how long it would take, you said you didn't know. "Then give me the address of the bar you are in now, and I'll join you."

"You might come for nothing," you said. "You might come only for the two of us to return together."

"That's good enough for me," I said.

I was sick of being in the house or in the small courtyard surrounded by tall walls, plastered with orange dirt and crowned by a roll of barbed wire. Unlike the other places you had lived in, this was in a central area. It was enough to take two steps outside the gate and I was in one of the busiest junctions in Kampala. Hundreds of motorcycles whooshed past me, a constant stream of students flowed from the university campus down to Wandegeya market, mixing with people coming from the city in search of the minibuses waiting at the end of the line, in the huge unpaved parking lot. On both sides of the boulevard, at the ground floor of buildings, there were shops with clothes, domestic appliances, graduation gowns, restaurants offered cheap meals out of big cauldrons, while on the edge of the sidewalk, women sold fruits and vegetables, among children and beggars.

In the past you had lived in residential areas with quiet streets and two or three story houses, where after a while people got used to me: the neighbors sharing our courtyard, the shopkeepers, the waiters at the terraces where I could have a coffee and read while I waited for the day to pass and for you to finish work. Here we didn't even have neighbors. The flat was located at the back of the owner's house, with a separate entrance and courtyard, and the gatekeeper wore a black and blue camouflage uniform and a gun. He didn't speak English and spent his day slouching on a chair, with his gun leaning on the wall, watching loud videos on his phone. Every time I came out onto the terrace, I felt like we were locked up together. From the street came the noise of motorcycles, occasional quarrels in Luganda, ibis cries that sounded like lambs bleating, and hours of rhythmic music from the nearby church that became increasingly urgent as the day advanced, accompanied by the thundering voice of a pastor who seemed to announce the apocalypse. Although the inside of the house had a modern design, with a bar, a spacious living room and art on the walls that you had chosen yourself, you seemed not to enjoy being there either, as you only came home to sleep.

You gave me the address of the bar and told me to take an Uber, which meant a car, not a boda-boda motorcycle. It was after seven; it was dark and after nightfall the chances of having an accident on the unlit street increased. Then you called back and said Francis would come get me. "What should I wear?" I asked before hanging up.

"Whatever you want," you replied, but not in the voice meant to reassure me that whatever I wore was all right, but in the irritated tone you used lately, although I had explained to you that it was enough that I was white, I didn't want to stand out even more for being inappropriately dressed.

I put on some tight jeans (like I had seen other women wear) and a white T-shirt with a golden-green inscription that I styled with glittering jewelry and high-heeled sandals, and I tucked an additional sparkling necklace in my bag, in case it turned out I was underdressed.

Francis arrived on foot. He lived in the area. I insisted on calling the Uber myself. I needed to prove that I could do things on my own. I put the pin on the map and waited for the driver to call me so I could explain to him exactly where I was. It wasn't clear to me whether GPS wasn't accurate in Uganda or if this was a leftover habit from the time when there were no digital maps and people found their way using physical references—a junction, a supermarket, a gas station—the way it was during my first visits.

"Gebaleko, sebo. Django oncime Bativa Road, behind Ham Shopping Centre," I said mixing Luganda and English. "Ntegerize." I am waiting. I knew the word because it was the title of your first hit single, a love song.

The gatekeeper opened the two locks and let us out. The street was dark, but the headlights of a car parked in front of the gate let us know that the Uber had arrived. We got in the car and Francis said there was someone else we needed to pick up, a friend of Julius, Moses. I wondered if it was the same Moses you had told me about the previous night, how he had gotten drunk and grabbed a girl by the arm and pulled her towards a boda-boda, insisting that she come back with him to the student hall, until you had had to step in and free her.

The car passed the check at the entrance of Makerere campus and stopped by the boys' student hall, a massive brutalist building that I had seen when I walked around the campus with Francis, and you said you would join us, but didn't. Now, in the dark, all that was left of the building were the lit-up rectangles of the windows. Moses opened the door and took the seat next to the driver. Francis shook hands with him, I asked him if he was a student, what year and which major, but he replied curtly, so I let him be and Francis started asking questions about me.

Your mom had finally invited me to dinner. Francis laughed. "So Mommy Namukasa is coming around".

I laughed back. "Yes, and it only took six years."

Francis said what he always said when we talked about your mother. That she was difficult, and she intimidated him as well, but once she knew me, there was no reason for her not to like me. It turned out he had been right. While you retreated to reply to some urgent emails, under the pretense that she was taking me outside to show me the damage monkeys had done to her garden, your mom sat me down on the terrace and subjected me to a long questioning about me and my family in Romania. She wanted to know how I saw marriage, what I planned to do in Uganda, if I wanted children and at what age. She told me I had to understand I was going to marry not a man, but a culture, and African culture is very different from European one, and I said that what she calls European is actually Western culture, while the world I come from has more in common with Africa than she imagines. My parents had also opposed our relationship and refused to meet you—but I didn't tell her that. In the end, she got up and hugged me, and we came back into the house where you hadn't moved from your laptop. It had been an important moment, the last obstacle in the way of our life together, and I was so immersed in the telling of the story, that it was only when the car stopped and three people exited that I remembered Moses was with us.

The Uber drove off and we were left in total darkness. I called you and you told us to enter what looked like the courtyard of an industrial building. In the distance we could see the light from an open door. You came to meet us, took my hand and gave me a brief kiss on the lips, even though you didn't like public displays of affection, which were not customary in Uganda, but a remnant of our life in Europe.

The bar was a repurposed industrial hall and I asked you if it was the one in the pictures. In London we had seen many spaces like this one; then they had started appearing in Bucharest, then you had found one in Kampala. You sent me pictures of it with the caption: *I found the hipster headquarters.* You said it was the hall in the pictures, your office was right across the street, you came here almost daily, there was a bar, a food court, an art gallery, a shop with clothes made by local designers and a space meant for parties. Beyond the wall of galvanized steel, decorated with stencils of palm tree leaves and wild animals, I could hear drums, guitars, a choir led by a resounding male voice. You said that was Julius; he was responsible for the music at a church meeting.

You led me to a chair and told the bartender to take care of me, but instead of a stranger, Isaac emerged from behind the bar. He hugged me over the counter, asked me when I had arrived. You hadn't told him I was in town. "I know," I said. "He likes to surprise people." A few months prior, when Crested Crane Records had offered you the position of Creative Director, you had called to ask my opinion. You weren't sure how Isaac was going to take it and wondered if accepting would mean selling out. But wasn't that the dream? To work in the underground music industry until you were good enough for the mainstream to want you? The fact that Isaac was there, in the bar you frequented, seemed a good sign. He said he was still making music; this job was only to make some extra money. You said you were leaving Isaac and me to catch up and sat down at a table with two women I didn't know.

When we lived in London, we had discussed how in patriarchal societies like the ones we both came from, a woman risks being seen not for who she is, but for who she is in relation to a man, and neither of us wanted that. I appreciated that you introduced me with my name and profession, "Diana, writer." It was a different starting point for a conversation than if you had introduced me as "Diana, my girlfriend." I knew this and I knew I had to be able to stand on my own two feet when it came to socializing.

Next to me at the bar was Karim, a young hip hop artist that you had just finished recording. He watched me inquisitively, probably wondering about the white girl acting so friendly towards Isaac. I told him I liked his music. I had seen him perform at Sofar the previous Sunday with you and Julius. He said he had noticed me too. "There was little chance I would have passed unnoticed," I laughed. I was sitting between Francis and him, on the other side of the bar Isaac was making me a drink, and I could feel the three men focused on me, asking me questions about my stay in

Uganda, but instead of their interest in a foreign being I would have preferred your interest in me.

I excused myself, got my drink and walked over to you. I placed a hand on your shoulder. You invited me to sit down and introduced me to the two women. They greeted me coldly, especially one of them, who was tall and robust. She pursed her lips and looked at me with her eyes half-closed. You told me that they were working at the art gallery and you said that they should give me a tour, that I was a fan of contemporary art. The smaller girl said *sure* and it seemed to me like she wanted to get up, but she stopped when she met her friend's gaze. The other one gave me a look that was either bored or pained, I couldn't tell, and asked me to forgive her, it had been a long day, and she had a headache. "Sure, no problem." We stayed in our seats. It got quiet. The smaller girl cleared her throat and asked me where I was from and what I was doing in Uganda, but as I was talking, I could see the other girl with her head thrown back, looking left, then right. I had never come across such animosity, at least not in your circles, and I wondered if it was because I was white or because I was your girlfriend.

Julius came out from behind the stenciled wall, and everyone stood to greet him. He was dressed in black boots, white jeans and a khaki silk tunic that was only buttoned at the neck, revealing a white vest underneath. A gilded peacock shone on his chest, hanging from a thin chain attached to the collar of his tunic, and round, gilded-frame glasses gleamed on his nose. We hugged. He took my hand and raised it, forcing me to do a pirouette. "Such understated elegance, I love it." I laughed, delighted.

Julius was hyped after the gig and talked animatedly, about the show, about the people in the choir, about the things he still needed to do: packing up the equipment, getting his money. A small crowd gathered around him: Francis, Karim, Moses, and others I didn't know. I sat down and finished my drink, exchanging smiles of genuine sympathy with the smaller girl seated across the table from me. She had her legs crossed and lightly swung a golden-braceleted ankle and every so often threw her long red braids over her shoulder. The other girl had stood up and was listening to you and Julius.

Eventually, we visited the art gallery. Francis hadn't seen it either, nor Karim, nor Moses. Behind the stenciled wall lay an ample hall lined with containers that housed commercial spaces with their shutters pulled down. The tall girl pulled up one of the shutters, revealing the window of the small gallery. "She not only works here, but she is also a painter," you said, and I wondered if she had made the painting at your house, which you had told me that you had had to buy from the owner of the gallery without the knowledge of the artist, who hadn't wanted to give it to you because *you didn't want it enough*. While the tall girl explained the paintings to Julius and Moses, I walked along the walls and tried to remember the signature on that painting at your house, whether it was anything like Winnie, what I thought was the girl's name. You were sitting on the chair behind the desk, with your legs stretched out and your hands on your stomach and a familiarity that made me want to gasp for air. "What do you think?" Francis asked me. I couldn't tell him the truth.

I was glad the group decided to go to Other, one of the hot stops in Kampala that attracted both Blacks and whites.

"Is Winnie coming?" I asked you.

"Vinnie," you corrected me a bit too sharply.

"Is Vinnie coming?"

"Yes."

We stood in the parking lot discussing how to distribute ourselves in the cars. Isaac couldn't come; he was working. Moses didn't want to come, but Julius said it was out of the question and assigned Moses a spot in his car. Francis and I were riding with you. Vinnie and her friend said they were coming with you too. Karim had to ride with Julius.

Vinnie opened the door of your car in my face, blocking my access, and climbed into the passenger seat. I crammed in the back with Francis and the other girl, wondering if I was going crazy or if there really was something wrong with the way you were both chattering in front, enveloped in an almost tactile intimacy, and only once in a while you remembered to throw a joke to us at the back, to which only the small girl replied, while Francis and I sat in an embarrassed silence.

Or maybe it was the fact that we had a long-distance relationship, and I was aware that I was missing out on the small victories and annoyances that made up your everyday life, but which at the end of the day didn't seem important enough to be communicated in intercontinental conversations. It was normal for you to have friends, including women, with whom to unwind and vent at the end of the program. After all, it was my friends in Bucharest I called when I wanted to complain about an email from my publishers, or moan that I had put in a red T-shirt with the whites. Maybe it was only my insecurity and frustration at the fact that we were living our lives separately that made me jealous of your relationship with Vinnie.

"This is where I got robbed," Francis said, pointing to a spot in the dark. "About two weeks ago, I was going home and the boda driver suddenly swerved left on a path and two guys jumped me. They took my wallet and my phone and hit me with a metal bar." He rubbed the back of his head.

You didn't say anything. You had probably heard the story already.

"What kind of boda was it? Had you ordered it through Safe Boda?" I asked.

"No, I picked it up by the side of the road."

In front of the club, the parking was packed. You found a spot at the far end and everybody got out. I said I wanted to leave something in the trunk and you stayed behind with me.

"What do you need to leave?"

"Nothing. I just wanted to be alone with you for a minute."

You laughed, pulled me close. You kissed me.

"You only kiss me in the dark."

"I kiss you when I feel like it."

"You kiss me when no one sees us."

You loosened the grip of your arms enough for me to pull away a little, but you didn't let go of me.

"What's going on?"

"Does Vinnie know we are together?"

"Of course. Why do you ask?"

"She doesn't like me."

"Why do you say that?"

"Have you seen the way she acts with me?"

"No."

"You should pay more attention."

You put your arm around my shoulders, and we walked into the light. Vinnie and the small girl were waiting for us on the path to the club. Before reaching them, you stopped and kissed me one more time. Your hand continued to rest on my shoulder, and I entwined my fingers with yours.

"Have you been here before?" I asked Vinnie and her friend.

"No."

"How about you?" the smaller girl asked.

"I have."

I had been there once before, a few days prior. Your habit of going out to clubs was a new development, something that had appeared in the half year since we had last seen each other. You weren't crazy about dancing. You usually liked bars with live music, but you had started frequenting Other for the EDM nights and the eclectic playlist, with music from Europe, Africa, Asia, and the Middle East, and because you liked to observe people. When you agreed to take me with you, you said you were nervous, that you didn't know whether I was going to enjoy it because Julius and Francis didn't. You usually went there on your own. We had sat at the bar, while you explained to me the groups. Expats that worked for embassies and international NGOs, young people that were there volunteering at charities or churches, backpackers with a brazen carefree air, businessmen with gold watches and undone ties, shady uncategorizable individuals. Next to us at the bar sat Black women with short tight dresses and sparkling jewelry running down into their cleavage, who were thinner and less shapely than the full-bodied women who usually acted like divas in other the places we went to. You told me those women were there to pick up white men. Some asked for money up front—"You mean prostitutes?" I asked, and you shrugged. "If that's what you want to call them,"—others were more discreet, expecting presents and the payment of certain expenses. "But don't worry, there are just as many men here to pick up white women. On this issue, there's gender equality," you laughed.

I looked around. "How can you tell who they are?"

"They have dreadlocks."

Indeed, Ugandan society sanctioned long hair in men, but around the bar were a lot of guys with dreadlocks, cornrows and braids, bright shirts and beaded bracelets that came closer to white people's idea of African people than everyday Ugandans. "Aren't there normal people too?" I asked. A white woman with blonde hair caught in a loose bun, dressed in jeans and T-shirt, sat next to a Black man with a crewcut, in jeans and a shirt—an outfit not dissimilar to yours; he kept his arm on the back of her chair in a gesture of casual intimacy, while they both conversed with a Black woman with an afro. I wondered what we looked like, whispering at the bar with our heads close together.

"Of course there are normal people," you said. "They're just not as interesting to watch."

We had such a good time that at one point you even agreed to dance, and the blonde woman with her partner and their friend came and formed a circle with us.

When we arrived at the club, you removed your arm from my shoulder to look for your wallet. Vinnie and the smaller girl waited behind us. You were greeted by the bouncer and the woman collecting the entrance fee, who said something in Luganda that made you laugh uneasy. You paid for all four of us, then I saw you slip the bouncer and the woman an additional banknote, another new development.

Francis, Julius, Moses, and Karim were waiting for us inside. They had found a table with couches next to the DJ podium. You said you were going to the bar. You asked me what I wanted to drink, then asked the other girls, too. It seemed like they were on your bill that night, as Ugandan social norms demanded, it was the men who paid for the women—I just didn't get why it was you who had to pay for all of us.

I grabbed you by the hand and whispered in your ear: "Will you let me buy you a drink? You've paid for my entrance."

You smiled. "Okay."

We headed for the bar, making our way through the crowd on the dance floor, then among the tall tables where the women with modelling bodies and the men with expensive whiskey bottles were seated. Two waiters in black and white uniforms passed us pushing a cake on a cart. They stopped in the middle of a group of white people and the music changed to Happy Birthday. The birthday girl screamed and hugged her girlfriends. The waiters lit the candles. Somewhere a champagne bottle popped. The people around were singing and clapping. At the end of the bar there was a pool table that attracted all the backpackers and suspicious characters, and beyond it, the terrace with rows of plastic tables waiting under colorful paper lamps. Other was designed according to Western standards, but without falling into any of the cliches about African bars: no animal prints, no tribal patterns, no mural paintings of sunsets in the savannah. The area with the bar, the fancy tables and the dancing floor was covered with a wooden structure pierced by the trunks of jacaranda trees and decorated with lamps of perforated metal, while the floor was made of stone slabs and strewn with violet jacaranda flowers.

You ordered two beers for Vinnie and her friend, while I ordered a beer for you and a cocktail. You knew the bartender. He watched me inquisitively, but you didn't introduce us. When we got back to the table, you squeezed yourself in between Julius and Francis, leaving me to take the only remaining seat, next to the small girl, on the same couch as her and Vinnie.

"Sorry, can you tell me your name again? I didn't catch it."

"Michelle."

"Diana."

We shook hands.

The couches were arranged in a semicircle facing the dance floor and I was sitting at one end. Michelle was the only person I could talk to, but she was leaning back and away from me, plastered to Vinnie, who was frowning at the dance floor. She took a swig from the beer and said to Michelle:

"Black men are stupid." She spoke loud enough for me to hear it. "They drool over white women not realizing it was colonialism that taught them white is beautiful. They are brainwashed."

She glanced at me, then returned to surveying the dance floor.

I didn't know how to react. Usually, the women around you were your friends or the girlfriends of your friends who extended a premise of sympathy towards me based on your feelings for me. What was I supposed to do now? Come to you and tell on her? Inform her that Romania hadn't had colonies? That I was a different kind of white? That what the two of us had wasn't about any of that, but about mutual understanding and human affinity? Normally I would have agreed with her, I was a fan of the Black is Beautiful movement, but this wasn't a debate, this was an attack.

I got up and said I was going to the bathroom. I crossed the pool table area, then the terrace with its empty plastic tables, all the while trying to calm down. My cheeks were burning, my heart pounding against my chest, and for the first time, I felt like I didn't belong there. The queue for the women's toilet extended all the way out. In front of me, two women were laughing loudly and joking with the men coming out of the men's toilet and washing their hands at the outdoor lavatories. One of the women had her hair gathered at the top of her head, where it exploded into a bouquet of tight blonde curls, and a long red dress that hugged her curvy body. The other one had short hair, a thin curl stuck to her cheek and a low-cut silver onesie. They both seemed in the grip of an alcohol-induced frenzy. I went into a cabin, lowered the toilet lid and sat down. I needed a place to fall apart without anybody watching, but it wasn't long before someone knocked on the door. I flushed and left the cabin. I washed my hands and looked in the mirror. My cheeks were bright red, the whites of my eyes were made pink by a filigree of red veins.

"I love your hair," said the woman in the red dress, smiling at me from the other lavatory.

I couldn't help smiling.

"Thank you. I love your hair too."

"Is this your natural color?"

"No. I dye it. Are those your natural curls?"

She laughed.

"No. I have to use shitloads of products to get them to look like this."

"Well, I've always wanted curly hair."

"Well, I've always wanted straight hair."

We laughed.

"That's life for you, isn't it?" she said, fluttering her hands to shake off the water, and then she walked to her friend who was waiting for her on the path.

Francis watched me on my way back to the table. It seemed he had been expecting me. You continued to talk to Julius, not letting on that you had noticed my return or my absence. Moses was listlessly eating a pizza—and I struggled to imagine him grabbing a woman by the arm and pulling her towards a boda-boda. Vinnie was still frowning, Michelle still small next to her. I said I was going to the dance floor, and Karim jumped to his feet. Michelle said she was coming with us. I would have liked you to come as well, or at least show that you had heard me.

The music was Bon Jovi, Psy's "Gangnam Style," Radio & Weasel, Backstreet Boys, Bjork mixed by Omar Souleyman. White people cheered for some songs, Black people for others, Asians for others. Some songs got everyone cheering, others got no reaction. Karim was a born entertainer: He danced with Michelle and myself, without coming too close to either and paying equal attention to both. He even had enthusiasm and energy left to interact with other dancers, men and women, who rallied in a big circle around us. At one point I saw you, Francis, and Vinnie advancing towards us through the crowd. You joined us and Karim started dancing in a self-mocking way that you and Francis immediately picked up, then Francis came to dance with me, and Karim was dancing with you, and Vinnie had her arms around a stranger's shoulders and the woman in the red dress and her friend in the silver onesie came over and put me in the middle. They were dancing provocatively in a way that reminded me of my nights of showing off with my girlfriends in Bucharest. Then the woman in the red dress whispered in my ear: "We have a friend who wants to meet you." She moved aside and a man took her place. He had dreadlocks, a wifebeater and an unbuttoned shirt with tropical flowers.

"I have a boyfriend," I said quickly.

"Where is he?"

I looked around and saw you talking to Vinnie.

"Why isn't he dancing with you?"

I didn't reply. I came over to you. Vinnie continued to say something in your ear. You laughed, then said something back. I stood next to you rummaging my brain for something to say, something funny. Eventually you noticed me.

"What's going on?"

"Some guy hit on me."

"So?"

"I told him I have a boyfriend."

"And if you didn't have a boyfriend, would you have accepted? You should have told him you aren't interested."

I went to the bathroom again, but this time I didn't go into the cabin. I went straight to the lavatory, soaked my hands in cold water and passed them over my neck and forehead. I looked in the mirror. What was happening to me? I had been to Uganda countless times before and I had never felt so uncomfortable, so confused, so unwanted. Was it your new job, the new social life, the new friends? Was it my fear of moving to Uganda?

I came over to you again.

"I need to talk to you."

You followed me to the terrace. We sat at a table. I wanted to take your hands into mine, like we did when we had difficult conversations, but from your position, leaning back on the chair, holding the beer with a hand, you didn't seem open to the gesture.

"Look, I don't know what's happening with me tonight. I am not okay. I need you. Can you stay with me? Can you not leave me alone anymore? I feel like you keep leaving me alone."

You said okay. We came back to the dance floor, and you started dancing with me, but you didn't look like you were enjoying yourself. I had proven that I couldn't handle myself. This was your biggest fear when it came to our relationship: that moving to Uganda, I would feel alone and lost and all my unhappiness would be on your shoulders.

The intro to Tupac's "California Love" started playing and I moved away from you. I went to dance with Karim who was standing in the middle of a circle of people, and rapping to an invisible microphone. I knew the lyrics, I had listened to hip-hop when I was a teenager, Tupac had been my idol. I started rapping too. Around us, people were cheering and bouncing their palms in the air.

When it got to the chorus, I went over to Vinnie and said in her ear: "I used to listen to a lot of hip-hop growing up. In the country I come from, we didn't have Black communities, and I didn't understand half the things Tupac was talking about, but somehow his music spoke to me."

She looked at me opaquely.

"I think art has this ability," I went on, "to touch something in us even when we don't understand the context, because it appeals to what is human in all of us, beyond skin color or the culture we come from. But you are an artist too. I think you understand this."

I thought I could almost see sympathy in her eyes. She nodded: "I do."

I felt myself regaining balance.

When we went back to the table, you sat down next to me. Moses was where we had left him, with the barely touched pizza in front, and Julius was by his side bearing an exasperated expression. You leaned over the table and said something to Julius, who straddled Moses and moved closer to you. You leaned over the legs of Michelle and Vinnie to hear him better, while on the other side of the couches, Moses, Karim, and Francis looked bored and ready to go home.

Over your back, I tried to catch Michelle's eyes. I wanted to ask her if she did other things apart from working at the art gallery, but she was immersed in her phone. In the meantime, you kept your elbows on her thighs, and your forearms on Vinnie's, and I felt something swelling up in me. How could you touch them so casually when you couldn't even hold my hand in public? Michelle got up and left, and you moved closer to Vinnie and continued talking to Julius. I was again at the end of the couch, by myself. On the other side of the table, Francis waved me to come sit next to him. I smiled and shook my head, I was fine. Now you were talking to Vinnie and her face was completely lit up. There was nothing wrong; it was normal for you to be talking to other people. I did not want to be the paranoid girlfriend. Then you took Vinnie's hand, removed her bracelet, put it on. A simple black beaded bracelet. Why couldn't you have just asked for it? Why did you have to take her hand? And then I caught sight of Julius looking at me and what I recognized in his eyes was, without a trace of doubt, pity.

I got up and didn't know where to go, to the pool table, to the terrace, to the bathroom. I needed to do something, to walk, to run. I headed towards the exit and out onto the path to the parking lot. The street in front of the club was empty, no boda boda in sight. I opened Safe Boda and searched for a bike. The app scanned the area on a radius of five minutes away, ten minutes, fifteen, twenty, thirty. Nothing. Across the streets the silhouettes of some giant trees were black against the sky, and from their crowns I could hear the flapping of wings from the kalolis. Beyond them, only darkness. Anywhere else in the world—in Bucharest, in London, in Valencia—I could have left. I could have wondered the streets alone, I could have taken a cab, the image of the city, of life carrying on beyond my problems would have helped me. But here I was completely reliant on you and that was my biggest fear about our relationship.

I know that you are not actually here. That this direct address is just a literary device. That you will probably never read this because the two of us have agreed not to send each other messages through our art. If we have something to say, we will say it directly. But you have left me no choice.

I came back to find you still immersed in conversation with Vinnie. And what did you still have to say to each other when you saw each other daily, and how come you had nothing to say to me when we hadn't seen each other in months? Vinnie was beaming a self-assured satisfaction, with half-lowered eyelids and a smile in the corner of her mouth. She was undeniably beautiful, with her statuesque figure, her hair braided and gathered in three tight buns aligned from her forehead to the back of her head, her shiny dark skin, her long legs sticking out from under her business skirt and her long fingers linked on the table.

I told you again that I needed to talk to you. You looked at me with a surprised expression but said sure. I went ahead to the terrace, but you stopped by the bar to get yourself another beer. When you finally sat down at the table, you tried to seem calm and open, but I could feel your underlying irritation.

"What's going on?"

"Do you like Vinnie?"

"Where is this coming from?"

"You didn't answer my question. Do you like Vinnie?"

"No."

"Would you tell me if you did?"

"If you don't believe me, why do you ask in the first place?"

"You act like you like her. She is cool, I can see why you'd like her. But I need to know."

"You're being irrational."

We looked at each other. You seemed honest and genuinely concerned for me. I knew I was falling apart, my cheeks were burning, I felt like crying, I hated feeling like that.

"I'm sorry, but this is what I'm feeling. I don't know what's wrong. It seems to me like you're not paying any attention to me tonight and that you like Vinnie. If there is something wrong with our relationship, I prefer to know. Please."

You seemed to be thinking, reaching a decision.

"Look, I don't want you to feel like I'm gaslighting you. I don't think I'm being any different from how I usually am. Vinnie is my friend and I like her, but not in the way you think. I'm sorry you feel this way. I don't know what to do. Let's get a third opinion."

I looked at you, confused.

"When you move here, we're not going to make it on our own. We need a support network, friends. You need other people to talk to apart from me."

"Okay."

"Who would you like me to call?"

"Julius."

I stayed at the table while you went to fetch him. Your offer was almost generous, giving me one of your friends.

When Julius appeared from the dance floor with his silk tunic flowing behind him, his gilded peacock and runway walk, I couldn't help smiling. He was smiling too, intrigued by the situation. But when he got close to me, I burst into tears. He took me in his arms—and I wondered how come you couldn't take me in your arms—and I told him about the evening.

"I feel like I'm going crazy. Please help me. How do you think he's been acting?"

"Yes, he hasn't really been paying attention to you," confirmed Julius.

I felt the ground return under my feet. I sighed in relief. I preferred to know what I was dealing with.

"Do you think he's in love with Vinnie?"

Julius proved himself to be a good friend to you and to us.

He said he didn't think you were in love with Vinnie, but that your new job was exceptionally stressful and in moments such as these it was easier to have superficial interactions rather than open up and connect to loved ones. He had been through something similar the previous year, when he had released his album. He had had the tour and weekly gigs in bars in Kampala and had had fights with all his friends, including you. Plus it was normal to take us a while to get used to being together after not having seen each other for months. It was just a difficult period. We had to be kind and understanding with each other, and we would overcome it.

I hugged him again to thank him. I asked him how he was faring after his difficult year.

"I'm okay. But you know life, there's always new shit."

"What new shit are you dealing with now?"

"Moses has cancer. Stage four. The doctors gave him zero chances. That's why I try to take him out of the house, convince him to eat. I don't want him to be alone."

I wish I could say that Moses's problems made mine seem insignificant. Of course I reevaluated my interactions with him, the moment he had listened to me talk about our future in the car, the way we had shown off on the dance floor, my teary self-absorbed back and forth. The situations did not cancel each other out, they added up: two obstacles in the middle of the road, impossible to ignore or overcome.

Julius went to get you. I asked him to communicate the verdict and as I listened to him telling you that you had been indeed ignoring me, I felt calm, even triumphant.

But you looked at me and said: "I just don't think I did."

*   *   *

Julius asked us to take Moses home. Karim got a ride from a friend and you went to help Vinnie find a boda boda. We waited for you for twenty minutes on the terrace, Moses, Michelle, Francis, and I. With my last forces, I tried to make conversation, while Francis tried to reply without letting on that he knew everything he knew.

In the car I reclaimed the seat next to the driver, but you were only looking ahead and joking with the people in the backseat. You seemed so likeable and funny. I wished you were like that with me.

Julius had instructed us to get Moses fruits and water. You stopped at a gas station and Michelle and Moses went in. Francis said he needed some fresh air and got out. I waited for you to turn to me. You were resting your arm on the open window and watching the gas station entrance. I touched your shoulder.

"Are we okay?"

"Yeah. Why wouldn't be?"

You stopped a late peddler with a woven basket on her head and bought a bunch of apple-bananas. You threw them in the backseat. When Moses and Michelle returned to the car, he said something in her ear, and she giggled. When you asked her about her address, she said she was getting off with Moses.

For the rest of the drive the three of you joked and laughed. There was so much good humor in the car, but I couldn't connect to any of it. You had cut off all connection.

*   *   *

Sometimes, in random moments, when I come out of the shower or I am cooking or I am walking the streets of Bucharest on my way to meet a friend, I still think about Moses, I wonder what happened to him. I know I could write to Julius or Francis, but it would be weird to ask about him, of all the people. And anyway, knowing wouldn't make any difference, would it?

CRISTINA CHIRA is a writer based in Romania who writes in Romanian and English. She holds an MA in creative writing from Birkbeck, University of London. She has published short stories in numerous Romanian magazines and anthologies, and her debut volume Raluca nu s-a culcat niciodată cu Tudor (Raluca Never Slept with Tudor) *was awarded Best Prose Book of 2023 by the Romanian publication Agenția de carte. "Each Other" is her first story published in English. It is part of her upcoming collection of short stories* Return Trip Bucharest–Kampala. *Cristina has lived in Romania, UK, Spain and, for short bursts of time, Uganda.*

Maybe Someday

Liz Rose Shulman

The black velvet top was sandwiched on a rack in between a bright yellow dress and a pink skirt with white stripes. I bought it at a secondhand shop around the corner from my second-floor studio apartment. It was the only one they had. I wasn't looking for anything specific when I walked into the store, but was only browsing, the way you do in your twenties when you look at clothes at secondhand stores. It's fun, it's an event. "Let's go secondhand shopping!" a friend suggests after you've had too much coffee with her. "Why not?" you say, because you have time. You see an oversized 1920s red and purple-jeweled brooch over here, or a small 1940s forest green hat with a mesh net across the face over there. Random stuff someone donated. You don't really think about that. Not yet. It's likely the people who owned these things are now dead, and a family member brought their stuff to the store in garbage bags. You don't think about any of that. You see some saddle shoes and pilled chunky wool sweaters with moth holes that smell musty, like old people. "Vintage," the store owner says with a smile. You don't think the people who wore these things had full, complex lives because you don't yet have to think about your life like that, *like a life*. You're in your twenties and you've got a lot of time.

The pink skirt with white stripes that was next to the bright yellow dress that sandwiched the black velvet top looked like a candy cane. It was a candy cane skirt. The black velvet top cost $2.50. It was a perfect cut. Sleeveless yet wide straps, a silver zipper all the way down the back. It was slightly cropped but barely, like when you'd stretch your arms above your head, you'd see a little skin near your navel. A classy amount of skin. It was a classy top. It had slits on the side about an inch thick. Good quality, too. The velvet was so soft, touching it reminded me of a man's face just after he's shaved. A little raw, totally smooth, not yet hardened from a day. When you think about that guy you don't think that he's had a whole life either, an *entire life*. You just think about that smooth face against yours. I tried the top on in the makeshift dressing room, a towel draped over a wire for privacy in the back of the store. There was no size, just a tag with $2.50 written on it. It fit me well. I paid and walked home.

When I got upstairs to my studio apartment, I put the top on again and stood in front of the mirror. With the jeans I was wearing, it looked good. I lifted my arms above my head and saw just a little skin by my navel and a tiny bit by the side slits. A classy amount of skin. It sure was a classy top. Perfect for a night out. As I looked at myself in the mirror I imagined living a different life, one I knew I'd never live.

It was the kind of top you'd wear to a dinner party on the Upper East Side in a pre-war apartment building with high ceilings and built-in bookshelves. The kind of party where people hold their stem wine glasses with their palms facing up in between their middle and index finger, as they walk and talk and move slowly but intentionally from eating dinner in the dining room to sitting on the sofas in the living room to having one or two side conversations in private in the den. Pre-war apartments have great layouts. They allow for multiple conversations between multiple people during a dinner party. The black velvet top would be great at a dinner party like that, where early in the evening you'd sit at a long chunky, very expensive wood table of maybe twelve people. They're interesting and smart and quite civilized, and they think you're interesting and refined, too, and smarter than they are, like when you tell them about the Edward Hopper exhibit you just saw at The Whitney, how you particularly loved his Washington Square Park series, you say, and they nod with envy because they haven't yet been, or when you tell them about *Blackbird,* the play you recently saw at the Belasco Theatre. Yes, you say, the one with Jeff Daniels and Michelle Williams. Yes, it did sell out, unfortunately, you add, and shake your head with disappointment for them as you hold your stem wine glass a few inches above the table with your palm facing upwards so it looks like it's floating. You're the kind of person who gets tickets for things. They're jealous because by the time they heard of the show, it had sold out. You tell them how, after the play, you saw Jeff Daniels getting in a taxi just in front of the theatre. You're in the know, you with your cute black velvet top. Everyone gets a little tipsy at parties like these and maybe a couple will make out in the small hallway by the bathroom but everyone's refined enough not to get obnoxiously drunk. Maybe a tad too much wine, a little slurring. They'll all feel fine tomorrow. The appetizers, mini bruschetta toasts with minced garlic and olives and fresh mozzarella balls spiked onto mini skewers with a tiny basil leaf, from an outside catering company that no one's heard of except the host, your friend. Of course, she tells you in the kitchen, I'll give you their number later. For your next party, she says, because you will have one, and you'll wear something great when you host, you think to yourself, like your black velvet top. You know that the woman across from you is envious of the wide sleeveless straps of your black velvet top and the side slits and the tiny bit of skin that shows only when you bend. That's a classy top, you know she tells herself. That zipper goes all the way down the back. Here I am at a dinner party on the Upper East Side in a pre-war apartment filled with bookshelves and perfect molding, you think to yourself, and no one knows I only paid

$2.50 for it at the secondhand store around the corner from my studio apartment.

The truth, of course, is that I've never been to dinner parties like that. And I've never lived in New York City. I've seen them in movies and thought, it sure would be great to have friends who invite you to their dinner parties in their pre-war apartments on the Upper East Side. But I haven't and likely won't start now because I don't have many friends and I don't really like the ones I do have and I'm just so tired all the time. Besides, I don't even know anyone who lives in a pre-war on the Upper East Side anyway.

When I took the top off after looking at myself in the mirror, after imagining a life I'd never live, I was going to hang it in the closet on the far right with the other pieces I never wore. But I didn't. This is significant. Bear with me. I hung it in between the center and the far right. It might sound trite, but it matters where one's clothing hangs in one's closet. I didn't hang the black velvet top in the far right with the other pieces I have that also represent a life I'll never live—the black dress with the three-quarter length sleeves and baby doll collar and the cabernet-red strapless dress with the satin bow at the empire waist. Instead, I put the black velvet top in between the far right and the center. It was an effort, I know now, to have a little hope. I'll likely never wear this, it means, but maybe I'll wear it. That's what hope is, a maybe. "I no longer love her, that's certain," Pablo Neruda writes in "Tonight I Can Write," "but *maybe* I love her." Like *maybe* the black velvet top will be different. Maybe it has more of a chance to be worn than the dresses that live permanently on the far right. And maybe if I wear it, I'll have that kind of life. To have hung the velvet top on the far right as soon as I brought it home from the secondhand store would have been a defeat, an admission of failure. I wasn't prepared to do that. But placing it equidistant between the center and the far right means perhaps someday. The locus of hope. *Maybe* someday, when I'll no longer live in a studio apartment by myself, and when I'll no longer smoke cigarettes, when I'll no longer be single. You know, someday, when I'll have friends in New York City who invite me to their Upper East Side pre-war apartment for a dinner party, the kind where people walk by and see us in the windows and we look so intellectual and cozy from the outside.

I'd been working nights at a neighborhood bar for a while, serving rum and Cokes and old fashions to regulars who got drunk, tipped well, and hit on me, when I bought the top. Once, I made out with one of the regulars who was twenty years older than me in the parking lot of the bar near my car after my shift. He looked like an aging Marlboro Man. We kissed sloppily for a few minutes, the flickering Budweiser neon sign our moonlight. That's not something girls who have strapless dresses like the one on the far right side of their closet do, I remember thinking. They're wooed, proposed to. They're certainly not making out with an old guy in Levi's in a bar parking lot full of gravel and cigarette butts. During the day, I attended grad school classes, learning to become a teacher—I eventually left the bar when I got my first full time teaching job—and tutored in the homes of rich kids and subbed at a nearby high school.

Those dresses on the far right, forget about it. They never had a chance to live anywhere but the far right. Those are the New Years Eve party dresses girls wore at the bar, dresses you wear when you're proposed to. Hang on. If it's a surprise, why would you be wearing a dress like that? Did you really choose to wear a cabernet-red strapless dress with a satin bow at the empire waist to go out to dinner? Who are the women who just happen to wear those dresses the night their boyfriend decides to propose? See, those are the kind of dresses you wear if your life was different. You buy a new one for each occasion. But I just couldn't throw them out. They're a foil to the daily clothes the way the pretty girl in high school is a foil to the ugly girl. One has a life and one doesn't have a life, and they need each other to exist in their respective roles. My life is the center clothes, the daily clothes—the part of the closet professional organizers call "prime real estate" because it's right there, in the center—of boring tops and pants that are fine because they are functional and generic enough for work. I have four pairs of the same black pants. I wear them with a semi-cute top and cardigan. Those are center closet clothes.

I wonder what it would be like to live a life where the far right dresses are the center clothes? Now that would certainly be a life! I remember the day I tried on the two dresses that live on the far right of my closet. When I put them on in the dressing room at the store I'm sure I knew I would never wear them. But they were so pretty and putting them on made me feel pretty, too. Especially the cabernet-red strapless dress. That's a special-occasion dress for sure. I took my clothes off in the dressing room that day, and stepped into the dress because it was strapless, and pretended I'd stepped into a whole new world, and then I remember thinking, who owns strapless dresses? And I shimmied my hips as I pulled the dress up and the satin bow on the empire waist was so delicate and girly but the strapless satin across my chest was womanly. And even though it was strapless it was high enough that I showed no cleavage. It was a classy dress. Like the classy velvet top. And then I tried on the black dress with the three-quarter length sleeves and noticed how it made my arms look longer and the baby doll collar made my neck look slimmer. So I bought both dresses and briefly imagined living a different life. But by the time I got home I was back to my life and I wondered why I bought them because I knew I'd never wear either one. Yet I couldn't bear to return them.

That would be an admission of not living a certain kind of life that I just wasn't prepared to admit, because maybe—"but *maybe* I love her"—I would be invited to a party someday where people wear dresses like that. I immediately pushed them all the way to the far right of my closet and they became the foil to the daily clothes in the middle. (By the way, the left side are jackets, in case you're wondering.) Since I already had clothes on the far right, it would have been a defeat to also hang the black velvet top there the day I brought it home. So that's why when I put it equidistant between the middle and the far right, I felt a flicker of hope.

What I'm really trying to say is that I'm well into middle age now, and I think I've spent much of my life waiting for my life to happen. It's not just the dresses and the velvet top. It's so many things: the martini glasses I bought for the dinner parties I knew I would never host, particularly while I lived in the tiny second-floor studio apartment and didn't even have a table, and only knew what a martini was because I made them for people at the bar; the plates I shoved in the back of my closet for just the right guy I would someday date; the skirt for when I would lose the ten pounds I wanted to lose. In the meantime, which is to say, while I actually lived my life, I settled for plastic cups and paper plates and average clothing.

I did wear the black velvet top once (which was more than I ever wore the dresses on the far right) to a bar not far from my studio apartment on New Years Eve. I had a crush on a guy who told me he'd be there. It wasn't really an invite. He'd only mentioned in passing that he was going, so I decided to go, too. I wore the top with dark blue jeans, black ankle boots, and a chunky red and black beaded bracelet. To be expected, girls pranced around in strapless dresses. I mean, if you're going to wear a strapless dress, New Years Eve is the night to do it. I thought the same about velvet. I stood around awkwardly trying to talk to the guy as he moved from group to group throughout the crowded bar. I realized around 11:30pm, when he failed to respond to my bad attempts at flirting that he really wasn't interested in me. I hid in the bathroom just before midnight and sat on the toilet as the crowd shouted the ten-second countdown in drunken unison. At midnight, I stood up, pressed my forehead against the bathroom stall in defeat and wondered what I was doing with my life, why I wasn't living a different life. At 12:30 I snuck out and called a taxi. The black velvet top didn't save me. I never wore it again, though I put it back in its place in the closet between the center and far right. Maybe someday, "but *maybe* I love her."

Another time, a few years after I wore the black velvet top once, I was at a grungy bar with some friends. Most of the people there were wearing T-shirts and flannels. It was smoky. Someone was playing Lynyrd Skynyrd's "Free Bird" on the jukebox. I was wearing middle of the closet clothes as per usual. Jeans and a top. Fine, functional. It was a square-shaped bar. Later, a small group of men and women, maybe six of them, entered the bar and sat across from us. They were all dressed up. One of the women wore a forest green strapless dress with a satin bow at the empire waist. It was just like the cabernet-red dress I bought but had never worn. Her green shoes had been dyed to match the dress. The men wore tuxedos. Clearly they had been at a wedding or graduation. My friends and I stared at them with our mouths open. They held themselves with an air of having been dropped into the grungy bar from another planet. They knew they didn't fit in and didn't care. They were above belonging. They held their glasses of wine with their palms facing up like weightless bubbles and sang the lyrics to "Free Bird" as though they were on a stage singing about traveling and things staying or not staying the same. They floated inches above their seats and their toes in their high heels were pointed like ballerinas. I bet the one who had the green shoes dyed to match her dress also was actually a ballerina who had pointe shoes dyed to match her tutus. One had perfect skin and a pouty lip and strawberry blond curls. I thought to myself, now that's the kind of woman who gets invited to parties at a pre-war apartment on the Upper East Side. Good thing she's got that strapless dress.

The velvet top didn't only live in between the center and far right of my closet. It lived somewhere in between my everyday life and my fantasy of the life I was missing. I kept it there for a long time. Finally, a few years ago, I admitted defeat and gave it away. It turned out it was a lot of pressure to put on a sleeveless velvet top that someone else donated a long time ago to a second-hand store. Then again, it's a lot of pressure to put on oneself, too, to always want one's life to be different, to not live your own life when you're living it, to one day be as old someday as the dead people whose clothes were dropped off in garbage bags at the secondhand store and wonder what you did with your life when you had it.

These days, I wonder what it would feel like to be old and to have been happy with your own life; which is to say, if I had worn the black velvet top a lot, so much that the velvet became mashed and worn, the zipper eventually broken, if it had lived in the center of the closet. What if I simply hadn't cared who wore strapless dresses and who didn't, if I had lived the kind of life where maybe might happen—"but *maybe* I love her." And I wonder what it would be like if someday someone in their twenties walks into a secondhand store after drinking too much coffee with a friend and sees that velvet black top in between the yellow dress and the pink candy cane skirt and thinks, now, whoever wore that top, that classy top with the wide straps and side slits and silver zipper all the way down the back, whoever owned that top, she really must have had quite a life.

__LIZ ROSE SHULMAN__ is the author of Good Jewish Girl: A Jerusalem Love Story Gone Bad, *published by Querencia Press. Her writing has also appeared in* The Wall Street Journal, The Boston Globe, HuffPost, Slate, Los Angeles Review, The Chicago Tribune, *and* Tablet Magazine, *among others. She teaches English at Evanston Township High School and in the School of Education and Social Policy at Northwestern University. She lives in Chicago. Visit her at lizroseshulman.com.*

Dog Gears

Katerine Ivanov Prado

He was a little older than the pictures on his profile, but not embarrassingly so. She thought he wasn't bad looking for his supposed late fifties, having retained a full head of hair and two rows of nice, albeit artificially bright, teeth. But he was blurry in the way all older white men were to her, like he could have been anyone.

Once they'd greeted each other with a limp one-armed hug, she settled in across from him at the table. They had arranged this introductory lunch after matching on the site, so that he could examine her before purchase like a racehorse and she could determine if he was planning on feeding her body to a woodchipper. His profile had said he was looking for someone educated, someone with whom he could have a real conversation. Under the *about me* section, he'd written a list of his other preferences: *looking for a well-manicured and intelligent young lady, between 20-25 years old. College educated. Preferably exotic.*

"You have a lovely dark complexion," he said in greeting. "Very nice skin. Do you tan? Or is this your natural…" He trailed off, skimming a finger around his water glass until it made a high-pitched sound, like cicadas rubbing wings.

"Nope," she assured. "This is just how I look."

"Good girl. I had a freckle on my back biopsied last year. Doctors kicked up a huge fuss, gouged a hole the size of a quarter. All that and it comes back benign! Not that I'm complaining," he complained. "Better safe than sorry, right?"

She nodded around bites of salad, aware she was supposed to be performing interest without alerting him of the performance aspect. As she chewed, he explained he was an executive for a national accounting firm, and flew in for monthly meetings in the mirrored glass building downtown. She had walked past it before, noted the dead birds littering the sidewalk.

"I know the website is, well, *gauche.* But this way, we both know the expectations going in," he offered conspiratorially, like, *you get it, right?* "I'd like to have someone consistent to spend time with when I'm in town." He was like most men who sought out this type of arrangement, distasteful of the explicitly transactional nature of traditional sex work, but too impatient or busy for the intricacies of maintaining a full out affair. He wanted an excess of convenience, a thin ghost of intimacy. The thing that felt the least like money for sex, while still being money for sex.

"Before I forget—" He pulled a tangerine box out from under the table and presented it to her. "Go on, open it."

She undid its ribbons to reveal one of those bulky, monogrammed Louis Vuitton purses, all buttery calf leather and gold-plating.

"Oh," she said. "You didn't have to."

"Do you like it?"

She did not. The overt branding made it the sort of panting symbol used to proclaim that you've become marginally less poor and she was uninterested in making such announcements. But the bag, of course, was not a bag. It was an outstretched hand.

"I love it." She leaned across the table and pressed her lips against his papery cheek, leaving the flushed imprint of her lipstick. "Thank you."

*　　*　　*

He asked her *the question* the next time they met, at a restaurant close enough to his hotel to intimate certain expectations.

"Why are you interested in this sort of thing? You know, with someone…older."

She chewed, pretending to consider her response.

"I'm just tired of dating boys who don't have their shit together. I'm looking for someone established." She lowered her gaze in a manner she hoped would project sincerity. "Someone I can learn from. Like you."

It wasn't true, of course. She'd made a profile on the site for the same, ordinary reason as every other girl: money. But the sort of man who had it in excess despised hearing about those who did not. He didn't want to hear about how she was the first in her family to attend college, how she'd finished with a dung heap of student loans and had, however foolheartedly, decided that a graduate degree would improve her job prospects. He didn't want to hear about how she lived off a paltry teaching stipend and had the credit score of a corpse, paid constant overdraft fees and worked demoralizing side jobs, sold her plasma and collected Safeway coupons like they were shavings of gold. The truth was that she wanted a softer life, a life without the suffocating, daily presence of *not enough*. It wasn't about the patina of wealth—she just wanted to catch her breath, even while aware of what this would require of her.

"Established," he smirked. "You're very diplomatic. I'm practically your age in dog years."

"How many people years is that?" she wondered. "Sorry, I've never had a dog."

"You've *never* had a dog? Not even like a family dog? *Really?*"

She laughed at his theatrical disbelief, as if she'd said she never had a roof over her head or clean water to drink. He was clearly the *dog is just god backwards* type of white person, and she was used to a different cultural mentality surrounding pets, where dogs were well-treated, but still considered animals and animals had a function. They guarded or herded or guided the infirm.

She wasn't accustomed to the idea of raising one like a baby, for the sole purpose of ownership.

In an attempt to further loosen up, she lifted her finger to order a third glass of wine, but he gave a small shake of his head. "I don't mind if you have a drink or two, but I'd rather you weren't drunk if we're going to..." He trailed off meaningfully. She thought his discomfort with her being intoxicated during sex was vaguely admirable, but then he opened his mouth again. "I'm not trying to babysit."

Outside the windows, the sky had grown swollen and cast iron black, promising rain.

"It's probably not safe for you to drive home in this," he said. A question, shrouded by plausible concern.

"Probably not." She agreed, already set on her answer. In preparation, she'd waxed and exfoliated and slathered herself with sandalwood scented oil. The kind of meditative grooming that functioned as a preemptive decision, an acknowledgement of where the night would end. They'd already ironed out the details, so as to avoid the mood-dampening, will-they-won't-they condom dance: She'd emailed him a PDF outlining her clean bill of health and proof of her contraceptive implant. The provision of documents had made it feel like applying for a passport.

There was something surreal about hotels, a neutrality that always made her feel as if she were acting out the parts of a script. It grounded her, in the elevator up to his room: the beigeness of the halls, the chirp of the key card. The anticipation in his eyes, which she realized for the first time were the pale yellow-green of wilted celery.

He kissed her, open-mouthed and filthy, and they met in the clumsy way that unfamiliar bodies do. She made herself soft and malleable and he adjusted her, moving her against the padded headboard, sliding a pillow under her hips.

"You can, uh, call me that," he said once he was fully inside her, and it was funny that he couldn't say it. "If you want."

She murmured the familial endearment he wanted to be called—that they *all* wanted to be called—in a put upon falsetto and he groaned like she'd winded him. She felt a quiet contempt for him that was surprisingly not incompatible with attraction.

After, he led her to the room's bath, running the tap until it was almost scalding. His pale, softened body flashed like a ship's sail as he helped her in and submerged himself behind her. They barely fit in the tub, even with her back pressed flush against his chest. Water slopped over the sides, flooding the tile. She wondered absently over who would have to clean it up.

He rubbed his bearded cheek against her shoulder, reaching around to lather her with the hotel's brand of shower gel. He took his time, using a soapy washcloth to gently trace her breasts and ribs, the softness of her stomach, between her legs. No one had ever bathed her before, at least not as an adult. It was somehow the most pleasurable and perverse way he'd touched her all evening, unsettling in its performance of intimacy.

She ghosted her fingers over his forearms, where his skin was thin, loose in a way she hadn't expected. She pulled at it until he told her to stop.

*   *   *

A few days later, a woman in a *Southwest Labrador Breeders* T-shirt knocked at her apartment door, holding a squirming golden puppy with a ribbon around its neck.

What am I going to do with it? she messaged him, attaching a photo of her new gift chewing up her kitchen table.

I think what you mean is thank you, he responded, with a winking face.

Thank you, she responded and she sort of meant it, because no one had ever gotten her a living thing before and there was a sweetness to it she wasn't prepared for. It would have been even sweeter if she'd ever wanted a dog.

*   *   *

At first, he gave her presents, not money outright, easing the path to explicit cash through the sort of gifts one would lavish on a real girlfriend. Once their schedule had been established—approximately one weekend a month—he set up an automatic deposit into her checking account.

"You can always come to me if you need more," he said. "I don't want you working too hard."

"I don't want that either," she agreed.

But when unpredicted costs reared their heads, she had difficulty stomaching asking him for more. In her search to avoid asking her parents for money, she'd found something that felt exactly like asking her parents for money. She never requested gratuitous amounts, and he never refused her: covering an increase in her tuition, two new tires, and a pricey trip to the vet after the dog ate a sizable amount of her down comforter and threw up a bouquet of feathers.

"What did you name him?" he asked, after she'd shown him a copy of the bill as a courtesy. *Trust me,* she hoped the gesture said. *I'm not scamming you.*

"Huh?"

"The puppy? The one I gave you?"

She'd only been calling it *the dog,* as in: *Can you please watch the dog? Can I bring the dog to class with me? Is the dog okay after all that puking?*

"Oh yes, I love him so much," she replied. "He's adorable."

*   *   *

They always met at his hotel when he was in town. Sometimes, she canceled class for him, haphazardly sending her students to watch presentations in the library. Sometimes, he forgot to tell her that he was busy, but she didn't and couldn't take issue with that. The unspoken rule of their relationship was that for a few hours at his beckoning, she became an amorphous, pretty entity without needs. She'd wait, sunning herself by the hotel pool until he returned, watching the fighter jets streak into the sharp jaws of the mountains, leaving silvery papercuts in their wake.

She didn't have a problem with this arrangement. As far as men went, he was not her worst, by far: He wasn't sociopathic or violent and didn't want anything too weird in bed. He even seemed interested in getting her off as a point of pride, eager with his hands and mouth. On one level, it was pure practicality: time spent for cash collected, making him the most lucrative job she'd ever had.

"Are you seeing other people?" he asked during one visit, splayed shirtless amongst the bleach bright sheets. The soft curve of his belly, nearly white enough to be indiscernible from the linens.

"Does that matter?" She lounged beside him on her front, paging through the room service menu.

"Well. I'd rather you not—I can, um, incentivize that."

She considered it briefly, but there was something repellent about the thought that he could purchase her fidelity. Apparently, she had limits, and this was one of them. Maybe she also needed to preserve the hazy, liminal space they inhabited between relationship and ownership.

"Don't worry. It's just you." She had technically been monogamous with him, albeit purely by accident; she was too busy at this point in her semester to take on either new clients or potential love interests.

"Thank you." He kissed her, long and lazy. "And uh, me too. I'm not going to…with anyone else."

"Okay," she said, placid. She wasn't sure if she believed him. Or if it really mattered, either way.

*   *   *

There were many things she didn't like about him. He was a caricature of a certain kind of man, made up almost entirely of talking points swiped from centrist news podcasts. He liked to reminisce in monologues about his mountain summits and fishing trips. His idea of pillow talk was asking her questions that were unsettlingly generic, like, *do you believe in God?* Whenever she said something he disagreed with, he'd squint like he was in sudden and tremendous pain.

"Do you remember where you were on 9/11?" he asked, during one of his post-coital inquisitions, his words chasing her body's slackening away with a stick.

"Kindergarten, I think," she answered, truthfully. "I remember they let us out of school early."

He rubbed his beard in false chagrin, like he was trying not to smile.

"Oh, man," he said.

To be fair, there were things she liked about him too. He was an unconditionally generous tipper to service workers. He never came to her with problems she'd be expected to solve. He gave affirmation constantly, a seemingly endless source of the word *good*. He kept his feet smooth and pumiced, soft against her legs. She liked the way he politely announced when he was going to come.

"I'm going to come," he said. "In, like, thirty seconds, I'm going to come."

"You don't have to give me an ETA."

"I'm trying to be considerate. Okay, shit, I'm coming."

Sex with him wasn't exactly enjoyable, but it wasn't bad either. It was a strange relief, abandoning the responsibility of one's own desires. Her body's unceasing hunger and complaints, quieted. Numb, but not unpleasantly so, like peppercorns, anesthetizing through brightness.

There was something satisfying about it, stranger and slipperier than pride. For a few nights a month, she became exactly what someone else wanted.

*   *   *

One visit, he accompanied her to the hotel pool, pulled a lounge chair right up to the edge and dangled a foot into the chlorinated water as he watched her swim. In the late afternoon light, he looked like a Hockney painting, flattened and domestic. His unbuttoned linen shirt exposing the pale expanse of his stomach, the flashes of blue-white incisors when he spoke. The sort of image that turned a bystander into a voyeur.

When he went to rise, she touched her pruned fingers to his ankle in disagreement. Gentler than she usually was with him, enough so to shock him into obedience.

She reached for her phone. He disliked her taking pictures of him, calling it her *generational preoccupation with documenting rather than living*, but this time, he allowed it. When she pulled herself from the water and showed him the photo, he was quiet for a long time, taking in his likeness.

"You really see me like this?" He stared and stared at his own softened face.

*   *   *

"You're going to age well," he told her, as he watched her clip her sweat-dampened hair up off her neck. "Could you leave it down?"

"What?"

"Your hair."

"No, the other thing. What does that mean, age well?"

"Oh, yeah. Sometimes you just know someone is going to come into themselves later in life. I feel like when you're forty or something, it'll all come together. Like your age will finally match who you are."

"Oh," she replied. "I think I've come into myself already."

"Sure," he placated, mouth curling up. He reached across the bed. "Get over here." The command yanked at strings she hadn't realized she was attached to, and she curled into him instinctively.

"Would you still want to fuck me, if I were forty?" She rested her head on his chest, curious if he would be honest in his answer. He rumbled beneath her, laughing like she'd told a fantastic joke.

"Baby, when you're forty, I'll probably be dead."

*   *   *

When her students acted particularly demoralizing, she liked to pretend he was one of their fathers. He could be, after all. She didn't know anything about his real life besides his job and the fact he had college-age children, revealed casually and then never touched on again, because her job was not to ask. There were many reasons men wanted to be called the name he liked her to use: the arousal that accompanied familial taboo, the intoxication of an overtly gendered dominance, the sweetness of daughters and all the affection they seemed to conjure. Some men liked it for reasons that were much, much worse. She decided she was not interested in figuring out which kind of man he was.

Her willful ignorance bloomed into a secret game she played. When her students ignored and talked over her, she'd just think: *I fucked your dad! I fucked your dad!* It made teaching far more palatable.

*   *   *

The first and only time they fought was a few months in, when she received a message while pulling into the hotel lot, informing her he wouldn't be available until late. Despite herself, she was annoyed. It was a forty minute drive to the foothills, and she was missing a lecture with a visiting scholar she admired. She knew her time was unimportant to him, but she thought she had sealed her indignation over it in airtight jars, stored in the cellar. She'd not accounted for the sheer resilience of her pride.

She posted up at the hotel bar and ordered their most expensive cocktail as she waited. He didn't like when she got drunk, called it unbecoming. Whatever, she thought. She didn't like him at all. In ten years, she told herself, she would be unbeholden to the world. And where would he be? Assisted living? She polished off four more drinks, billing them all to his reservation. By the time he finally returned, she was well on her way to belligerent.

"Finally," she greeted, disdain undermined by a hiccough. He took in her flushed face, the empty glass she'd brought up to the room.

"What's my one rule?" he asked, irritated. "What's the *one* thing I don't like?"

"I was bored," she responded. "You were supposed to be here hours ago."

"And you're supposed to be an *adult*. Adults don't need to be constantly entertained." He kicked off a shoe with more force than necessary. "I don't want to see you like this." She heard it in his tone, like he was sending back an incorrectly cooked steak: *This isn't what I paid for.*

His rejection opened up a small, mortifying part of her, the part that desperately needed to be wanted, and if that wasn't an option, used. She wished she were sober, so she could think of something eviscerating to say, so she could articulate all the ways she thought him pathetic. Instead, she burst into tears.

"I'm sorry." The words came out like she'd been ready to apologize all her life. "I'm really sorry."

"Don't cry," he instructed as he called her a car, which only made her cry harder. "Go home, okay? No man wants to deal with this."

Don't talk to me like that, she thought, but did not say.

The next morning, regretful of dismissing her company, he sent her a massive floral arrangement: lilies and roses, crowded by swathes of baby's breath. She returned from an early morning walk all cotton-headed and miserable—she wouldn't have even been awake, if it weren't for the fucking dog—to the vase on her doorstep. *Come back*, the note read, and she did, carting her bruised ego over the threshold like a reluctant bride.

That was the first time she really didn't want to sleep with him, but did anyway. It must have peeked through her schooled expression, because he stopped his rocking movements to cradle her face gently, like she was made of spun sugar. She wished he wouldn't touch her like that, with a concern that she couldn't deduce the integrity of.

"Do you want me to stop?" he asked. "We can stop."

She shook her head, because at that point, she really didn't. Because she would never again forget exactly what this was. Because even if she said, *yes, please stop,* she wasn't completely sure that he would—and that was a point from which they could not return.

"I can't do this anymore," she said to no one, while sitting with her elbows on her knees, perched on the toilet. A new, unsteady voice sprang from her mind in response.

Then don't do it, the new voice said. Testing the weight it could hold, like a foal. *Just walk away.*

She entertained the idea momentarily. Her newfound financial freedom was too intoxicating. No more minimum wage side hustles, swallowing her days. She could throw away the Safeway coupons.

She could settle her bar tabs and send her mother flowers. Having enough was an over-ripened fruit, disintegrating against her teeth and running down her chin. A sweetness that she would never get enough of.

She ignored the voice and flushed the toilet.

*   *   *

For the week of her spring break, he took her on a trip to Mexico. *Let me spoil you,* he texted, with a screenshot of their proposed itinerary. *You deserve it.*

She called a friend in her program, unsure if she wanted to be talked into or out of going. With her peers, she'd been fairly open about the arrangement, simply saying that she was seeing an older man who "took care of her" whenever anyone asked. They were accepting of this to the point of ambivalence; she was not the first graduate student to dabble in sex work and she certainly wouldn't be the last.

"Why *wouldn't* you go?" her friend asked. "Do you think he's going to kill you or something?"

"No, nothing like that." She didn't know how to explain her reluctance. She knew what they were when they were together, here in the hotel. She was worried that on vacation, under the sweet lull of elsewhere, they'd become something murkier.

"Okay, then I have another question—can you watch the dog?"

*   *   *

In Puerto Vallarta, they spent five days at an American chain resort. On the beach, her skin sucked up the sun, warm and greedy; beside her, he grew redder and redder like a boiled crustacean, until he gave up and sequestered himself to umbrella shade.

When the hotel attendants' gazes lingered on them, she burned with a fresh, insistent shame, unrelated to their age difference: He looked like all the other American tourists, and she looked like them. When they addressed her in clipped, customer service English, she withered, but did not correct them. *I'm sorry,* she thought, when he requested an extra towel or sent back an oversweetened drink.

I'm not like him, she wanted to insist in an attempt to assuage her own guilt, knowing that potentially made her even worse.

In the evening, they walked down a stretch of shore marked off by a hotel sign that threatened trespassers. The sand was warm and soft, giving way easily beneath her feet. A uniformed man in thick leather gloves patrolled the line of sun loungers, whistling periodically to call the falcons that circled above the resort to ward off pigeons and panhandling seagulls.

"This is where I'm from," she told him absently, nearly drowned out by the roar of the Pacific. "Well, where my family is from."

"Here?" he asked, bemused, as if he couldn't believe anyone inhabited this place for longer than a week or two at a time. They had not strayed from the Hotel Zone. He knew nothing of the shirtless boys, hacking open coconuts. The women who walked the length of the public beaches, selling whole fried snapper skewered on sticks. The water and gas trucks, announcing their presence each morning with a bullhorn. Those were hers, and she would not relinquish them from her heart's fist.

"Not here, here. From this state." She nodded towards the ocean. ""Do you want to go in? The water is so blue."

"No," he responded. "But go ahead."

She waded in, senses dulled by the cold, the salt. The meditative roar of the waves. Above her, the falcons cast a dark slash onto the water. She thought she saw a smattering of swimmers' caps out past the break, but when she strained her eyes she realized it was only a line of buoys, roping off the hotel's allotment of the sea.

On their last night in Mexico, he dug his fingers into her hips as she sat astride him, as if attempting to leave an imprint in still wet cement. "Please," he whispered under her, "please, please, please." She could feel his desperation, a thick humidity. She liked it best like this. Him, begging. Her, giving. A balanced call and response.

"Don't you wish this was our life?" he asked, after he'd announced himself. When he said things like this, she knew he'd convinced himself of some reverence that had bloomed amidst artificiality. It made her sad, although she wasn't sure on whose behalf.

"No," she said. He looked wounded, so she elaborated more gently. "You wouldn't like it as much if it was available all the time. Like how if you have too much of a good thing, it stops being good and starts being everything else."

"So wise," he teased, before growing pensive once more. "If only I'd met you thirty years ago."

She both loved and hated when he said this kind of thing. Loved the longing of *if only* and *years ago,* loved being the subject of the sort of wistfulness that tried to unravel time. Hated the dishonesty of it—of course he wouldn't want her if she were anything besides what he'd specified, if she had flaws and needs and plans of her own. The worst part was that he didn't even realize he was lying.

*　*　*

She ended things between them a few months later upon the completion of her graduate studies, offering him an assortment of repurposed phrases from breakup texts and letters of resignation: "I'm entering a different stage of my life, but I really enjoyed our time together. Thank you for everything. Wishing you all the best going forward."

He took it well, leaving the door between them cracked— "Don't hesitate to reach out, okay? I'm here if you need me." He only contacted her once more, a message sent late at night: *I think about you all the time.* She didn't respond, because who was he even thinking about? Not her, not really.

As expected, the deposits to her account stopped. She accepted a job teaching at the university full time, which paid a borderline livable wage. To supplement her new mediocre paycheck, she took the Louis Vuitton purse to one of the higher-end consignment stores in town. She'd looked up the retail value as soon as she'd gotten it and had almost thrown up. Forty-five hundred dollars.

The streets were deserted, the temperature too brutal for pedestrians. The dry season had stretched this place to its limit: without rain, the heat was almost absurd. A cartoon sun. She'd bought the dog those overpriced booties to protect its paws from the pavement. The rubber soles squeaked against the store's tile.

"Sorry—no dogs," the girl at the counter said, without looking up from her phone. "Policy."

"It's over a hundred degrees."

"Is it a service animal?"

"I'll be quick," she said.

The girl sighed, wiped her hands on her thighs like she was about to do something difficult. "It can't come in. You can tie it up out front."

She tied the leash to a post in the sliver of shade beside the door. The dog sat down immediately, pink boots splayed. Its tongue lolled out the side of its mouth.

"Selling or buying?" the girl asked when she returned.

"Selling."

The girl flipped open a binder full of laminated pages with pictures of zippers and authentication tags in microscopic font. She paused on a close-up of stitching and tapped the picture with a chipped red nail.

"Real ones have a cross stitch, like this. I guess I can give you twenty dollars for it. Or forty in store credit."

"Twenty?" Maybe she had misheard. "Like, two-zero?"

"Yeah. This is a knock-off," the girl said, not unkindly. "Didn't you know?"

Outside, the dog was waiting, stomach heaving like a bellows. She unwound the leash, overwhelmed by the quiet pull of its reliance. They walked two blocks before it stopped to shit in the middle of the sidewalk. She didn't have a bag to pick it up. The dog looked up at her adoringly, like it had accomplished something they could both be proud of.

KATERINA IVANOV PRADO's *writing has been published in* Narrative, Brevity, Catapult, The Rumpus, Joyland, Passages North, *and others. She has won the Narrative Story Contest, John Weston Award for Fiction, and the AWP Intro Journals Award, and has received an Elizabeth George Foundation Grant, a 50th Anniversary Fellowship from VCCA,* *a Mary Gibbs and Jesse H. Jones Fellowship, a LitUp Fellowship, and a Rona-Jaffe Scholar's Award from Bread Loaf Writers Conference. She obtained her MFA in Fiction at University of Arizona and is a PhD candidate in Literature and Creative Writing at the University of Houston, where she is the Online Nonfiction Editor at* Gulf Coast *and an Editorial Fellow at Arte Público Press.*

Animal Control

J. Stillwell Powers

Pauline spent most of her time dealing with domestic animals. Cats and dogs. Now and again, she wrangled fugitive cattle or goats escaped from the hobby farms in the hills north of the town center. Occasionally, she tracked a marauding raccoon or skunk. There were less enjoyable parts of the job. School visits. Town meetings. Paperwork in her little office at the municipal building on North Main. She had to put animals down. After sixteen years on the job, she thought she'd seen everything there was to see, trapped everything there was to trap, euthanized everything there was to euthanize. Then, one day in July, the calls started coming.

"Like a weasel on stilts," she said to Vicky, who stood, wrapped in a blue towel, by the dresser. "Slender in the midsection like a greyhound."

Vicky rooted through her underwear drawer. Her dyed-blond hair hung in wet strands over her shoulders. Glancing into the mirror atop the dresser, she said, "I've never heard of an animal like that."

Pauline crossed her legs on the mattress. Earlier that day, she'd collected a stray terrier living by the river behind the old Starling

Paper building. Some mud from the riverbank still clung to the hairs on her shin. She crossed her legs the opposite way to cover it.

"I figured the old lady was just lonely," she continued. "Looking for someone to talk to, you know? So, we walked her property together. We didn't find anything, but yesterday, I got another call from a woman on Mechanic Street. She described the same animal. A hairless dog with a narrow snout and green eyes. It was lingering in the pines, she said, just watching her little girl play in the yard."

Pauline paused for effect. The young woman did have a little girl on her hip as she spoke about the animal, but she'd fabricated the detail about it watching from the pines, just to give the story a little extra intrigue. Maybe it worked. Vicky hummed as she hiked up her underwear.

"And earlier today," Pauline continued. "This Puerto Rican guy calls and says it's a chupacabra."

"A chupacabra?" Vicky said, laughing.

"Who knows?" Pauline said, watching the way Vicky's shoulder blades shifted beneath the skin as she fastened her bra. "We might have a mythical creature on our hands."

Vicky laughed, and said, "Well, what do you think it is?"

Pauline had some ideas, but she thought Vicky might prefer the mystery.

"We're going to trap it to find out."

"We are?" Vicky said. "When?"

"Tonight," Pauline said. "I've got the traps in the van."

Vicky leaned toward the mirror, turned her head side to side, examining her face. She ran two fingers over the acne scars on her right cheek. She felt insecure about them, even though the insecurity never showed in public. Like the little blue cross she'd tattooed on her thigh with a sewing needle as a teenager, or the way she sometimes whimpered and kicked in her sleep, it was one of the little secrets Pauline kept about her.

"I wanted to go down the Roadhouse tonight," Vicky said. "There's a band playing."

"You're down there every night."

"Work doesn't count."

"The Roadhouse will be there next weekend," Pauline said. "A monster? You never know how long it'll linger. We'll make a date of it."

*   *   *

At St. John's Cemetery, Pauline parked the van beside the rusted crypt door in the hillside. She'd explained the reasoning behind the location to Vicky on the drive over. The first call had come from the old woman who lived on North Main, which ran along the cemetery's western boundary. The woman with the little girl lived to the cemetery's south. Finally, the man with the Puerto Rican flag hanging from the porch of his trailer lived on Garvey Street, which hooked around the cemetery's northeastern edge. Triangulate the calls, and the cemetery rested dead center.

With the trunk open and the overhead light glowing, Pauline examined the two Havahart 1080s. They were the biggest of all the traps owned by the town. Not quite big enough for a coyote, but perfect for a fox or raccoon. Vicky watched as she lifted the gate. She fiddled with the mechanism, checked the springs.

"The animal goes in," Pauline said, demonstrating with her hand. "They step on this lever and the gate drops."

She tapped on the pressure plate and the gate fell on her arm. Vicky nodded. She'd heard plenty from Pauline about animals encountered on the job, but Pauline never thought to tell her about the tools of the trade. To her, traps and catchpoles and chemical repellents were as common as flour and eggs to a baker, but she had to admit it was nice to have someone to listen as she explained the mechanics of the trap. The job could get lonely, though she never thought about it until Vicky came along.

After collecting the cans of cat food from the glove compartment, Pauline dropped them into the cargo pocket of her shorts, and said, "I'm thinking we put one to the northeast."

She pointed in the direction of the trailer where the Puerto Rican man lived. Then, she motioned toward the apartment building where she'd met the young woman.

"The other to the southwest."

Vicky said, "You're the expert."

As they walked the dirt road running the cemetery's edge, each carrying a metal trap by the wire handle on top, Pauline said, "Maybe it's just a cigarette-smoking raccoon?"

A smile darted across Vicky's lips and vanished just as quick. A little over a year ago, Pauline brought a PowerPoint presentation to the emergency shelter on South Main. A few of the residents had developed a relationship with a local raccoon. The animal had become so friendly, the director told Pauline, it took potato chips straight from the hand. In the shelter's common room, Pauline explained the ways animals become dependent on humans if they're regularly fed. They lose their natural instincts, risk spreading diseases to house pets and people. They could become aggressive if denied. As she spoke, one man raised his hand. In his other arm, he held a chubby baby wearing only a diaper. He wanted to know if raccoons smoked cigarettes. The woman sitting beside the man rolled her eyes. As the story went, he'd tried to give the raccoon a cracker, but it snatched his cigarette instead and scuttled off into the trees.

"I don't want to think about that place," Vicky said.

They continued along the bend in the road, their footfalls scraping against the gravel, with a backdrop of evening sounds, crickets and birds. The setting sun slung their shadows long over the earth. Laid beside Vicky's, Pauline considered her own shadow, their differences. She stood taller in her work boots, shoulders wider than Vicky's, hips squared by her cargo shorts. She guessed her own shadow could cover Vicky's entirely if she walked behind her. She shifted the trap to the opposite hand and watched their shadows merge as she stretched her arm across Vicky's shoulder.

"We always used to laugh at that story," she said. "I didn't mean anything by it."

*   *   *

Traps set, they returned to the van. The radio warbled low as they drank cans of Pabst Blue Ribbon with the windows down. Darkness draped the cemetery. Vicky smoked her Pall Mall Lights and talked about the Roadhouse. Glen had hired a cover band to play on Friday nights, bought a pizza oven to complement the grill and fry-o-lator.

"He's trying to clean the place up a bit," Vicky said. "I told him about this bar in Florida where I used to work. It had a big dance floor. I said he should move some of the tables at the Roadhouse and try it out."

"You think people would use a dance floor?"

"I don't know," Vicky said. "Glen liked the idea."

"I'm not saying it's a bad idea," Pauline said. "All I'm saying is this isn't Florida."

"No shit," Vicky said, sipping her beer. Beyond her window, the crypt entrance stood shadowed by the slope of the hillside. Rust showed through the green paint on the metal door, but the lock was new, made of stainless steel.

"What was the bar called?"

"Wild Bill's," Vicky said. "Cowboy bar in Okeechobee."

 Pauline laughed.

"Why are you laughing?"

"I didn't know there were cowboys in Florida."

"Cowboy bars all across America," Vicky said. "It's a make-believe kind of thing."

"Well, if there aren't any real cowboys," Pauline said. "What makes it a cowboy bar?"

"The barstools are shaped like saddles," Vicky said. "There's a set of longhorns on the wall, horseshoes on the bathroom doors that say *Dudes* and *Dames*. There's a country western band and line dancing. They do these rodeo nights where they bring in a mechanical bull. They have a contest for free drinks where they put one of the pretty young bartenders on a chair and people try to lasso her."

Pauline imagined the bar with its longhorns and saddle seats, pictured Vicky seated in a chair with her ex-husband tossing a rope at her. Vicky refused to speak about the man, but Pauline imagined him with big hands, powder blue eyes, and a dimple on his chin. Maybe Vicky wondered about Pauline's past, too, though she never asked. Not that there was all that much to tell. Other than the neighbor girl who she'd kissed when she was eight years old out of a shared curiosity inspired by John Travolta and Oliva Newton-John, there was only Sam. They'd met in a biology class at the community college in Prescott. When they weren't studying, they spent most of their time wrestling beneath the blanket on Sam's bed in the little studio apartment where she lived.

Maybe they were in love, Pauline didn't know. It was nearly twenty years ago. She did, however, remember a gathering Sam brought her to at the college. The event was attended by other students, many of whom had dyed hair and piercings, T-shirts printed with complicated logos and acronyms. Everyone painted picket signs for a protest they planned to attend in Boston. Pauline didn't know what to write, so she helped Sam on a sign that said, *Out of the closet. Not going back.* Either way, the relationship fizzled shortly after Pauline failed to show up for the protest. It wasn't painful. Sam had plenty of friends—she didn't need Pauline—and Pauline convinced herself it was easier to be alone.

She brushed Vicky's hair aside and said, "Don't worry."

"Worry about what?"

"I don't know," Pauline said. "Anything."

For a long while, they drank their beers and listened to the radio, talking in short exchanges about the future. Pauline wanted to put a patio behind the house so they could relax in the evenings. Vicky wanted to look into getting a loan for a vehicle. The darkness thickened across the cemetery.

Vicky's cell phone buzzed. She dug it from her purse, looked at the screen, and sighed as she opened the van's door.

Pauline said, "Who is it?"

Vicky closed the van door behind her without an answer.

She claimed they were bill collectors looking for money whenever she denied calls. Occasionally, Glen called to offer a shift at the Roadhouse, to ask questions about an incident the night before, to remind her to do something she'd forgotten. Once or twice a week, her mother or her son, Trevor, called from Florida. Same as her ex-husband, Pauline had no idea what her son looked like, but she remembered the sound of his voice. Timid, tired sounding. That day at the emergency shelter, after Pauline gave her presentation, Vicky had followed her onto the front porch. She asked if she could please use her cell phone. The shelter only allowed residents one call a day from the office line. She needed to talk to her son.

That day, standing on the porch in full sunlight, there was something about Vicky that drew Pauline's gaze, like a hummingbird to bee balm. She wasn't young anymore, though something about her appearance had fooled Pauline. Her hardscrabble beauty was the kind you might find far north, where the earth is all pine and granite. Later that night, as Pauline filed paperwork in her office, her cellphone rang. It was Trevor. He said he had missed a call from this number and asked whether it came from his mom.

A night bird sang from the trees at the cemetery's edge. In the distance, Vicky lingered at the bend in the road where it rose toward the heart of the cemetery. The light of her cell phone screen carved from the darkness the easy angle of her jaw, wisps of hair by her ear. She looked ghostly in a way that made Pauline imagine her existing in two places at once. And out there with her, some kind of monster. It could have been watching from the pitch of headstones as she spoke into her phone, lifting its snout to inhale her smoky scent on the breeze.

When Vicky dropped into the van's passenger seat again, she said, "Trevor's in some kind of trouble."

"What kind of trouble?"

"He needs some money."

"How much money?"

Vicky looked at her phone in the palm of her hand like she might find the answer there on the blackened screen.

"Take me to the Roadhouse," she said. "I'll see if Glen will lend me until payday."

"I'll give you the money, Vicky," Pauline said. "How much do you need?"

"Please, Pauline," Vicky said. "Just take me."

The cold calm of her voice kept Pauline from pushing the issue. She turned the van and drove in silence down the cemetery road, replaying in her mind the last spat they'd had about money. Vicky's first week working at the Roadhouse, some drunk had palmed her butt as she passed with a platter of drinks. She promptly dropped the platter to the floor and shoved the man, who slipped in the mess of beer and glass. Still on his ass, he held up a bloody palm to Vicky, and said, "Look what you did, you bitch."

Just quit, Pauline told her that evening after Glen sent her home. She made enough money for both of them dealing with animal problems for the town. Vicky could stay home and write the memoir she always talked about. She could start a garden to grow vegetables and herbs. They could rescue a dog, and Vicky could spend her time looking after her. In the ensuing argument, Vicky said she didn't need a sugar daddy. Pauline knocked her glass off the table, stood so quickly her chair fell over. She shouted, *Is that what you think of me?* Vicky rented a room at the Travel Inn, and Pauline lived alone again for three days. And even with all of that time to think in silence, she couldn't figure out why she'd lost her temper.

The Roadhouse parking lot was lit in amber streetlight, packed with pickups and sedans. A row of motorcycles leaned against their kickstands by the establishment's cinder block facade. A banner with a beer logo hung above the door, *Live Music Friday*. Pauline parked between a pickup and a motorcycle.

"How long are you going to be?" Pauline said.

"Ten minutes tops," Vicky said, opening the passenger door. "Glen's tending the bar and it's busy. He won't want to chit chat."

As Vicky slipped inside, the boom of the music barreled into the night like a passing train and faded again as the door swung closed. Pauline eased back in her seat, angled another can of beer from the cardboard carton between the seats. She drank, watching the moths and mosquito hawks circle the light tacked to the corner of the building, resenting Vicky the fact she'd gotten her way after all.

*   *   *

In the thirty minutes Pauline waited in the van, she finished twenty-four more ounces of Pabst, watching drunks swivel in and out of the Roadhouse for cigarettes. As she pushed her way through the bar's door, the music stirred the drunkenness in her head the way hatchery fish roil their vats while feeding, muddling her vision as she searched the room. The air inside was thick with the odor of onion rings and stale beer, dented by the subtle musk of cheap cologne.

As she approached the bar, she spotted Vicky in the rear, standing beside a booth table occupied by people Pauline didn't recognize. Maybe she'd seen them around. Two men, one wearing a mustache, and a woman with hair feathered at her temples. Townies. Vicky tilted her head back and laughed at something the man with the mustache said, though the sound of it was hidden beneath the clamor of the band. The lead singer sang a lyric about a broken heart. A cymbal crashed and Pauline took the furthest seat at the bar, closest to the rear wall where the pine shelves held the liquor bottles. A taxidermy buck hung overhead. A set of green Mardi Gras beads and a pair of black panties dangled from the right antler. Through the gap between the two men seated just around the bar's corner, she watched Vicky sip a highball. Jack and Coke. She always brought home the sour scent on her breath after her shifts.

Glen tossed a paper coaster on the bar, leaned forward, and shouted over the music and clatter of voices, "What'll it be?"

She scanned the liquor shelf but decided against the idea since the work van was parked in the lot. They still had to drive back to the cemetery and collect the traps. She ordered another beer. As Glen returned to the cooler, Pauline watched Vicky across the room, forward-bent, talking to the people at the table.

"Open a tab?" Glen said as he set the bottle on the coaster.

Pauline said, "I'll pay for Vicky's drink, too."

He tilted his head.

"She works here," he said, and a moment passed before he grinned like he understood something secret Pauline was floating his way. "Wait? You're Vicky's roommate, aren't you?"

Pauline stood from the barstool, took a long pull from the bottle, and wiped her lips with the back of her hand. She fished her wallet from her pocket and slid loose a twenty. Handing it to Glen, she said, "Keep it."

The band stopped suddenly at the end of their song, and only the hum of drunken voices remained. A thread of laughter, a hook-fingered whistle, some half-hearted applause. Vicky lifted her glass to drink, and in the low light from the shaded lamp above the table, Pauline could tell it was mostly water now, a few fragments of ice floating inside. When she reached the table, she laced a finger through the belt loop at the back of Vicky's jeans. She tugged hard, and Vicky rocked in her direction.

"Hey," Vicky said. She blinked slowly, drunkenly. "I was just getting ready to leave."

The table was crowded with glasses, empty beer bottles, a half-spent pitcher with a ring of foam hung around the rim. The woman seated at the table said, "Vicky told us you two are out hunting some kind of wild animal."

"I bet it's a coyote," the man with the clean-shaven face said. "I bet you deal with a lot of coyotes."

The band started up again. A slow song, something lovers rock to with arms resting on each other's shoulders. She scanned the faces around the table, observing their shapes but not really seeing the features, and the memory came on like a premonition. The scent of ammonia still brewing in the hollows of her sinuses. A specter, lingering through the years, unnoticed until now.

"A few years ago," Pauline shouted over the music. "I got a call out to this old farmhouse up the state line."

The woman leaned in, and the men seemed equally willing to listen.

"This lady had so many cats I had to call in Prescott and Levon Animal Control," Pauline said. "The smell was so brutal it brought tears to my eyes. Thirty-six cats. The bathtub was filled with litter just as hard as a rock. Cats lounged in the cupboards, in the sink, on top of the refrigerator, in the television wires. In the bedroom, a dozen sat on the mattress."

"Sad," Vicky said. "I never understood how people—"

"Let me tell you something about sadness," Pauline interrupted, refusing Vicky her eyes. "I'm up in the bedroom with all of these cats staring from the bed. The smell is just unbearable, so I go open the window for some fresh air. Down in the backyard there's a pen, split rail fence built off an old pine shed. So, I go down there. And I find this horse, lying on its side. Like a skeleton, all its bones showing. Ribs. Hips. These dark eyes rolling around in its skull. Its hooves look like giant corkscrews in the dirt. They had to be three feet long, and so heavy the horse couldn't lift its legs to turn away from me."

The woman stared down into her liquor glass. The man with the mustache blinked at the other man and shook his head.

"When I came back out front where the police were standing with the woman, she glared at me with this hateful look in her eyes. If we were alone there, she would have killed me. And she screams, *You can't take them! They need me!*"

Pauline turned her gaze on Vicky. Her eyes looked glassy, like she was thinking about something far off in time or distance. In the heart of the bar, a few couples had gathered on the dance floor. Pauline tried not to think about what it would be like to dance with Vicky while everyone in the barroom watched them sway.

*   *   *

The van's engine idled low at the traffic light on the south side of the Pocumtuck River. In the passenger seat, Vicky stared through the windshield. The red glow of the traffic light glistened in the tears on her cheeks, but she made no sound.

"What are you crying for?" Pauline said.

Vicky said, "I just want to go home."

"We need to pick up the traps first," Pauline said. "If someone hasn't already walked off with them."

The light turned green, and Pauline eased the van onto South Main. They continued through the channel between the brick mills, across the bridge that carried the pavement over the river, past the town common and the Shady Vale Diner. As they rounded Water Street, Vicky said, "They're my friends, Pauline. Why did you have to go and tell them that awful story?"

"It wasn't for them," Pauline said. "I want you to know what it's like trying to love you."

Vicky laughed.

"Why are you laughing?"

"I'm not some neglected animal," Vicky said. "I don't need you to rescue me."

"You're mixing up the meaning."

Vicky wiped her tears away. She lit a cigarette and shifted her body toward the window. Outside, the town rushed by, smeared light in the darkness.

As they passed the emergency shelter on East Main, Pauline eased her foot off the gas pedal. The first floor windows of the ramshackle Victorian were darkened, but a few windows on the upper floors glowed, rooms occupied by drifters passing through. The night she returned to the shelter to let Vicky talk to Trevor on her phone, she waited on the front steps while Vicky paced in the moonlight. The meaning of the conversation was lost in the distance between the yard and the porch, but Pauline could sense the growing tension in the cadence of her speech, the intensity of her pacing. Eventually, Vicky stopped dead in her path and stared at the phone before dropping to her knees. By the time Pauline had crossed the yard, she was on all fours, her head tucked between her elbows, face buried in the grass. Pauline rubbed her back to soothe her crying, shushed her the way she did sometimes as she approached frightened animals with the catchpole. She knew right then she couldn't let her go back to the shelter. She needed to be with someone who could love her.

"Why don't you just have him come stay with us?" Pauline said.

"Who?" Vicky said. "Trevor?"

"I'll buy the ticket," Pauline said. "He can take the spare bedroom."

"What would he want to come here for?"

"To be with you."

In the ensuing silence, Pauline pictured the boy standing at a window with the curtain pulled aside. The disappointment at the sight of an empty street. Those days alone in the house after Vicky vanished, Pauline felt it a thousand times—that sinking in the gut—the feeling came on whenever she dragged herself out of bed. It baffled and frightened her. What was so different about the aloneness she felt in Vicky's absence? In nature, nothing. She'd been alone her entire life.

Across the cemetery, the moonlight gave the gravestones the look of a cityscape in miniature. The headlights carved the terrain from the dusk, glinted off the lock securing the crypt door as they passed, and Pauline steered the van along the bend in the road. As she continued up the hill, the light drew names and dates from the smooth stone faces, illuminated plastic flowers and knickknacks, souvenirs left by the living for the dead.

In the heart of the cemetery, where the road looped around the flagpole, she shoved the transmission into park. She shut down the lights but left the engine running.

"Will you come with me?" she said.

Vicky sighed and opened the passenger door.

Guided by the glow of Vicky's phone, they wove through the night, sidestepping headstones, the earth mossy beneath their feet. Pauline's thoughts wandered among the dead, just a half dozen feet below. If they could speak with the living, what would they say about loneliness? Knowing what they know about how things come to an end, what would they say about love? Pauline was trying to pin some kind of answer against the beer-slicked surface of her mind when Vicky suddenly stopped. Her hand gripped Pauline's wrist.

"There's something in that trap," she whispered. "I just saw it move."

Pauline pushed forward, and as they approached, a hum unraveled in the dark, like the sound of an engine fading in the distance. A pause for an in-breath. Upshifting, picking up speed.

Pauline leaned forward, straining to see, and the animal snarled before snapping at the wire cage.

"My God," Vicky said, hooking her arm with Pauline's, pulling herself close. "What is that?"

"Use your phone," Pauline said. "Shine the light."

Inside the cage, a slender frame, pale gray skin stretched taught over bone. The scent of infection. Emaciated and afraid, there was nothing mythical about the creature, nothing monstrous about her.

"It's a fox," Pauline said. "Looks like she's got mange."

"What's that?" Vicky said. "Some kind of disease?"

"Mites," Pauline said. "They live under the skin."

Pauline examined the yellow-brown scales grown around her ears, across her shoulders, the opened abscesses along her ribs. Wide, green eyes staring, the fox brandished her teeth. A pitiful growl unwound from her throat while the muscles in her hind legs trembled, too exhausted to fire.

"Can you help her?" Vicky said.

It's never easy to tell. Sometimes, with a little care, a ruined animal can be redeemed. Other times, it's best to end their suffering.

After the police carted that old woman off to the station for processing, Pauline and the animal control officers from Prescott and Levon returned to the shed. The horse moaned when they entered, reared its head and threw it down against the dirt, corkscrewed hooves knocking together like wooden blocks. The other officers looked to her for an answer, even though they all knew what had to be done.

J. STILLWELL POWERS was born and raised in rural New England. He is a graduate of Greenfield Community College and Amherst College, and holds an MFA in Fiction from the University of Oregon. His work has been supported by the Fine Arts Work Center and the Elizabeth George Foundation, and has appeared in Willow Springs, The Florida Review, *the* Southern Indiana Review, *and other journals. He currently lives in South Texas with his two children and is pursuing a master's degree in clinical mental health.*